JAPAPA

A novel by

Gary Schmelz

Three teenagers in the Bahamas face
death from an evil voodoo priest.

For information regarding permission, please write to:
info@barringerpublishing.com
Barringer Publishing, Naples, Florida
www.barringerpublishing.com

Design and layout by Linda S. Duider
Cape Coral, Florida

ISBN: 978-1-954396-46-3
Library of Congress Cataloging-in-Publication Data
Japapa / Schmelz

Printed in U.S.A.

TABLE OF CONTENTS

Crooked Island District Map

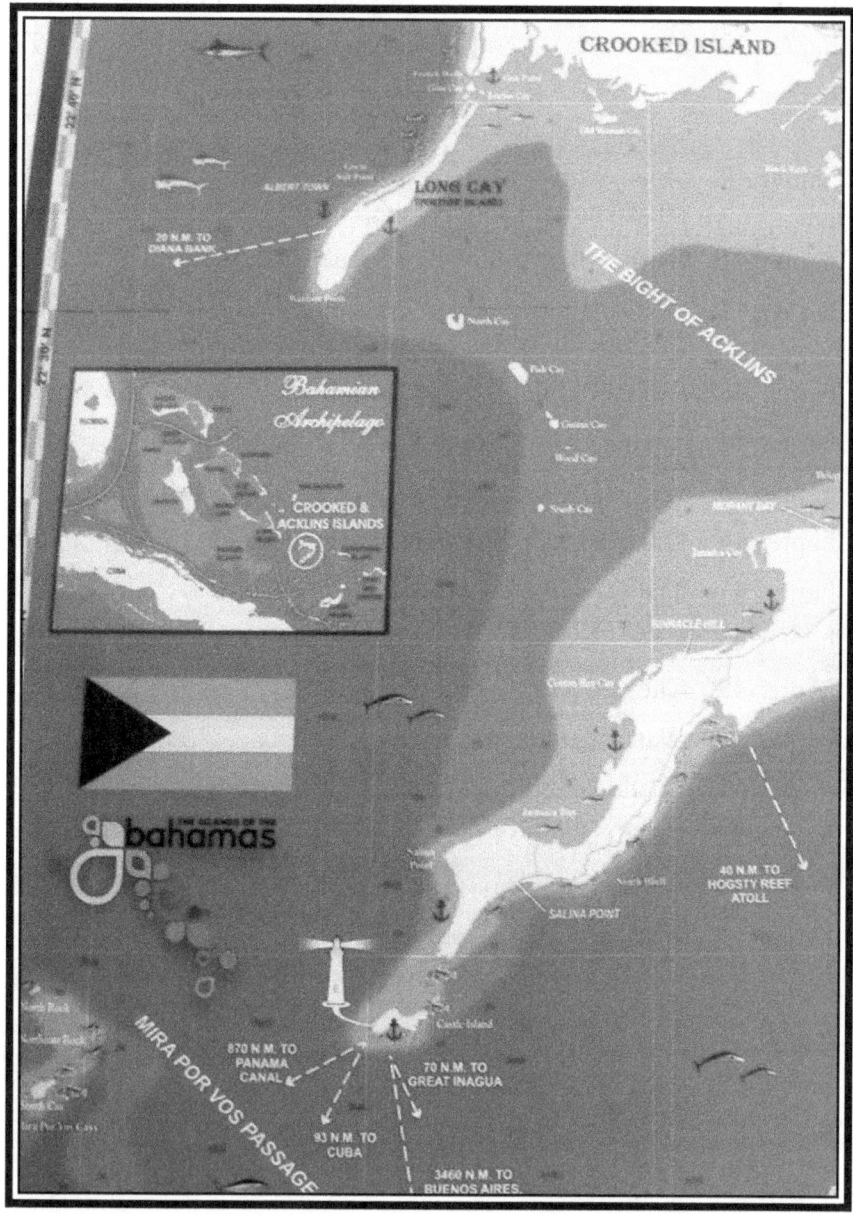

Bahamian Dialect

for	fer
into	inta
man	Mon
to, too	ta
than	dan
that	dat
that's	dat's
the	de
then	den
them	dem
there/their	der
there's	der's
there're	der're
they are	dey are
these	dese
they	dey
they have	dey've
they will	dey'll
this	dis
those	dos

GARY SCHMELZ

ACKNOWLEDGMENTS

My sincere thanks are extended to Lindsay Addison, Molly Godley, and Theron Trimble who were kind enough to read earlier versions of *Japapa* and offer constructive criticism and encouragement for bringing this endeavor to fruition. To my wife and buddy, Bernice, I offer my appreciation for all the help she provided in making this exciting publication a reality.

PROLOGUE

The Island of Haiti

OCTOBER 2006

"*Japapa dwe mouri*! Japapa must die!" The angry mob shouted in Creole and shook their fists as they pushed their way forward, crushing the palace's iron gates beneath their feet. Presidential guards had long since abandoned their posts, leaving no one to prevent the massive crowd from spilling into the courtyard.

There wasn't much time left. The burley voodoo priest nervously surveyed the angry mob that was gathering beneath his window. It had taken Japapa many years to assume his position of power and wealth. His peasant mother had left the countryside and journeyed to Port-au-Prince looking for a job. Her family was too poor to take care of her and she was hoping to begin a better life. She found a job working as a waitress at a local hotel where she met Japapa's father. It turned out he was the owner of the hotel and Japapa's mother told her son that it was love at first sight. But his father saw things differently. When she got pregnant, he fired her and threw her out onto the street. Life was hard after that. She was forced to rent an apartment in the inner city and clean houses for rich Haitians and Americans. After Japapa was born, things got worse. His mother worked eighteen hours a day to make ends meet and often they went without food. Japapa resented being poor and especially hated the way rich people looked at him whenever he went with his mother to clean houses. From an early age, he wanted to become rich and powerful. His mother said he could do that by getting a good education, but they never had enough money for him to go to the better schools where that could become a reality. Then someone suggested he become a priest. Not a poor Catholic priest like his mother went to pray with, but a priest identified as an *ougan* who practiced voodoo. After school, while his mother was at work, he studied with a nearby voodoo priest who practiced black magic. It turned out the priest's magic was very powerful and soon Japapa learned to use it to gain control over people. In certain instances, he found out that he could employ the dead against people who threatened him. When his mother discovered what he was up to, she pleaded with him to give up his studies with the priest. She said it would lead to his downfall. But he scoffed at that idea and soon his powers with black magic came to the attention of their country's provisional president, Boniface Alexandre, who said he needed someone with these talents to control the people who were trying to overthrow the government. Praising him for his skills, the president asked if he would work for him as head of his secret police. Delighted by the offer, Japapa took charge of the nation's secret police and for years he ruthlessly subjugated the people to his will. Using torture and black magic, he soon had everyone under his control. The people feared him. And those that didn't were either killed or banished from the island. However, over time, a powerful underground movement began to develop, and as much as he tried, he couldn't suppress this uprising. It was this group, with its powerful allies, that had overthrown the government and was threatening to hang him.

Tightening his grip around the metal railing of the window ledge, a sigh of frustration issued from between Japapa's lips. Turning around, Japapa stepped into the palace's darkened interior where the demon, Baka, with two penetrating eyes, glared back at him. The creature generated no warmth, only the frozen chill of the afterlife.

"Who's their leader?" Japapa asked as he wiped the sweat from his wrinkled brow and shook his head in disgust. "I know I've seen him before."

"He's the son of a family you had abducted and imprisoned several months ago," Baka snorted. "His name is Claude Joseph."

"Ah, yes, now I remember." Moving closer to his companion, Japapa stopped and frowned. "He pleaded with me to save their lives, but there was nothing I could do. The police caught his parents inciting some locals to overthrow the government."

"It's a pity you didn't take my advice."

"Yes, you warned me he would become a threat. I should have listened when you told me to have him executed along with his parents."

A brief silence followed. Japapa reflected upon this moment of weakness and scowled. It was his second of two critical mistakes. The first was when he banished a high priestess from Haiti. The wrinkled old hag, with her horribly twisted nose, was known throughout the island as Mama Atabei. It was hard for him to imagine why anyone would name this hideous looking woman after the beautiful sky god's mother. What he feared most about her was her ability to use an exorcism to reverse the curses he had used against his enemies. He should have employed his charm to soothe the woman's enormous ego. Flattering her might have turned her into a willing conspirator and avoided the desperate situation in which he now found himself. It would have been easy enough to do but she constantly challenged his ideas, and when he could no longer take it, he lost his temper. Flying into a fit of rage, he ordered her captured, then chained in the hold of a cargo ship, and abandoned on a deserted island. As they carted her away, she promised to get her revenge. The hate he'd seen in her eyes made him tremble with fear. Now his skin crawled every time he thought about the priestess. The creation of such a powerful enemy left him no choice but to form an unholy alliance with Baka, the evil spirit of the afterlife.

Initially, the partnership with Baka made him extremely wealthy and powerful. Baka had granted him everything he asked for including an agreement to prevent him from getting old. No one was able to defy Japapa. Kings and presidents cowered before his six-foot-four frame. Then the priestess escaped. Some of her supporters had rescued her and she became the leading force behind his present downfall. Baka could do nothing to protect him from her powerful magic. The priestess summoned her followers to support Claude Joseph's efforts to oust Haiti's corrupt president. The young man began holding meetings throughout the country, inciting people to overthrow the dictator's regime and establish a democracy. The groundswell of resistance he generated eventually became too strong for the corrupt government to overcome, and Joseph was able to drive out Haiti's ruling family and dislodge Japapa from his position as head of Haiti's secret police. If he stayed in the country, there was little doubt they would hang him. His only choice was to flee his homeland. Next time, he would take Baka's advice and make sure those who threatened his survival were eliminated.

"Death to Japapa," the crowd in the courtyard shouted again as they began ramming the palace door with a large wooden log.

The president had already left Haiti and now it was time for the priest to depart. Looking over at his desk, he grabbed the large satchel he had packed earlier. It contained most of the money he needed to set up his drug smuggling operation. The last of the arrangements with his new business partners had been completed that morning, and if everything went well, he would return to Haiti even richer and more powerful.

"I gather you've made plans to leave the country," Baka observed.

The acrid odor from the creature's foul smelling body made Japapa's sensitive nostrils twitch. Yes, the priest nodded as he raised a handkerchief to cover his nose. "A boat is waiting for me outside Port-au-Prince."

"Have you decided where you're going?"

"Somewhere in the Bahamas. The out islands are isolated— not too many people snooping around. They're also close to the shipping lanes, so it'll be easy for me to smuggle in drugs from South America. My English and Spanish are good enough for me to conduct business deals with both groups. Do you plan to come with me?"

"For now, I intend to remain behind to take care of your enemies and prepare Haiti for your return. Our spirits are so intertwined, we'll never become separated from one another. Wherever you settle, I promise I'll maintain our partnership."

Rocks hurled from the courtyard below suddenly shattered the palace windows spraying glass throughout the priest's office. It would only be a matter of minutes before the mob stormed the stairs. The door leading to the main entrance had been torn down and he could hear the shouts for revenge rumbling through the hallways. Ducking behind some furniture to avoid the rocks caroming around the room, the priest tightened his grip around the satchel and sprinted towards the rear of the palace where one of his men was waiting.

"Beware of the old priestess," the creature cautioned Japapa as a reminder. "She's sure to be watching you."

Stopping briefly to wipe the sweat off his bald head, Japapa turned and shook his head with distain. "You don't need to remind me. I made that mistake once. She'll never get the upper hand again."

"Let's hope not," Baka snorted.

Exiting down the dimly lit hallway leading to the back entrance, Japapa felt a sudden chill run down his spine. Looking around, he thought he heard the faint laughter of the old priestess echo off the palace walls. Soon, he would be free of the taunts of Mama Atabei and be running his lucrative drug operation in the Bahamas.

Local Fisherman off Castle Island, South of Crooked Island, Bahamas

NOVEMBER 2006

His calloused hands pulled the last of the wire fish traps aboard his weathered fishing boat. Once again, the trap was empty. "Where are all de fish?" the tired, old man grumbled to himself. For over thirty years, he'd always caught fish in these waters. Now, none of the traps he'd set the previous day had anything in them. "Maybe dey were raided by other fishermen," he mumbled. But he knew that didn't make any sense. He hadn't seen anyone else in these waters for over a week. Frustrated by this unwelcome turn of events, he tossed the last trap overboard and decided to see if an extra day of fishing would bring better results. It meant another day away from home and another lonely night on the rugged shores of Castle Island, but if he expected to make any money and feed his family, he needed to give it one more try.

Turning on the boat's ignition, the aged fisherman raised his trembling hand to shield his eyes from the searing late afternoon sun and scanned the distant shore for signs of life as the sputtering engine propelled the leaky, barnacle-encrusted craft across the tranquil, pale blue water. Except for a gentle breeze, there was no sign of movement anywhere. The abundant bird life and the hissing hordes of small, silvery baitfish that usually occupied the shallow flats during the rising tide had disappeared. The only things he saw were tiny clusters of bubbles rising to the surface. At first, there were only a few, but by the time he reached the island's protected cove and anchored his boat, their numbers had increased dramatically.

The fisherman had heard others talk about seeing bubbles, but this was the first time he'd ever observed them. Too tired to be concerned about their mysterious appearance, he dropped the anchor, lowered his aching bones into the warm water and slowly waded ashore. The sun was sinking below the horizon and the cool night air began to chill the sweat that had accumulated on his wrinkled brow. A hearty meal of rice and beans and a good night's sleep were what he really needed the old man thought to himself as he trudged through the water.

Initially, the fisherman didn't notice the peculiar mist that had gathered offshore. It was the increasing hissing sound created by the mysterious bubbles rising to the surface of the lagoon that made him turn and watch. Never before had he seen anything like it. A dense fog soon blotted out the remaining light from the setting sun and gradually began to creep towards shore. Curious, he stopped to watch. It was a decision he soon regretted. Within seconds, the cloud blanketed him, sucking the air out of his lungs. Terrified, he opened his mouth and tried to breathe. It was fruitless. He was no longer able to suck air into his lungs. He needed to escape, but where? Then he remembered the abandoned lighthouse located atop a nearby hill. Pirates had used it as a navigation beacon when they wanted to retreat to the island after attacking ships. There was also a cave underneath it that shark fishermen used as a camp. Either might be high enough to let him get away from the suffocating cloud. Forcing himself forward, the fisherman stumbled up the hill, his aching muscles protesting each panicked step. Looking up, he finally spotted the cave entrance. It was no more than a hundred feet away. As the mist continued swirling around him, he prayed that he would make it there in time.

Castle Island, Bahamas, A Couple Weeks Later

"Do you think anybody lives on the island?" Japapa asked one of his crewmen. He and his men had been at sea several weeks since escaping from Port-au-Prince and still hadn't found a satisfactory place to set up a permanent camp. Anxious to begin his drug smuggling operation, he had relentlessly pushed his followers to find a suitable site but every island they visited was either populated with local fishermen or too far from the main shipping routes.

"I don't think so," his tall, lanky assistant, Peter, said. Peter had been captain of Japapa's secret police in Haiti and the priest trusted him with his life. It was Peter who helped him escape from the palace and arranged the boats they needed to get to the Bahamas. Without Peter, he was certain he would have been captured and hanged.

"There was a small village at Salina Point on the north end of the island," Peter added, "but it was abandoned a long time ago. A lighthouse was built at this end but is no longer occupied. You can see its faded exterior against the skyline. I've ordered the men to lower the dinghy. I suggest a few of us go ashore and take a look."

"The shoreline looks pretty rugged," observed Japapa. "Is there a place where we can beach the dinghy?"

"I think so," one of the other crewmen said and pointed to a protected cove a short distance away.

"Good. Let's head in that direction. I'm sick of living aboard this crate."

Boarding the dinghy, Japapa carefully studied the rubble-strewn shoreline looking for signs of life. It wasn't until he was about two hundred feet from the beach that he caught sight of a small fishing vessel anchored in the shallow turquoise lagoon.

"Just our luck," Japapa grumbled. "I was hoping the island would be deserted."

"It doesn't look like anyone's on board," Peter observed. "Here, take the binoculars and look for yourself."

Peter was right, Japapa thought after he focused his field glasses. *There was no sign of movement aboard the vessel.*

"Go alongside and see if you can rouse someone," Japapa demanded.

Several shouts failed to summon anyone as they pulled up to the bow of the weatherworn boat. Suspicious, Japapa instructed Peter and one of his crewmen to board the vessel and check things out. When they returned and informed him no one was on board, the priest nodded his head and frowned.

"It seems strange that anyone would abandon her," Peter said as he lifted his Miami Dolphins cap to wipe his brow. "It doesn't look like there's been anybody aboard for several days. Moldy bread and other food are still on the shelf inside the cabin."

"They're probably on the island," another crewman suggested.

"Perhaps," Japapa said, "but I don't like the looks of things. Why would anyone let their food spoil? I suspect there may have been foul play. Head for the beach but stay alert. I don't want to be caught off guard."

They brought their dinghy ashore and proceeded up the beach but no one felt at ease. Dead land crabs littered the dune area and the island seemed completely devoid of birds.

They pushed their way inland and headed up toward the cliff via a narrow, overgrown trail covered with thorny greenbrier vines and stunted acacia trees. "Not even mosquitoes," one anxious crewman panted. "You'd think you'd at least run into some of those bloodsuckers."

"Over here!" Peter shouted and motioned the others to hurry.

Clamoring over some slippery rocks covered with vines, Japapa and the remainder of his crew were greeted by Peter's horrified stare. Near some bushes, not far from where Peter was standing, they saw the body of an old fisherman. He had died in agony. His mouth and eyes were open wide and his right hand was wrapped around his throat.

"W-what do you think killed him?" Peter stammered.

"I don't know." Japapa narrowed his eyes and knelt closer to the body. "There's something very wrong about this place. Take a closer look at the old man and tell me what you see."

For a moment, everyone stared at the fisherman. "I'm not sure what you're getting at," Peter said. Kneeling next to Japapa, he narrowed his eyes and ran his slender hands across the body. "Except for the fact that he died in extreme agony, he looks like any other dead person I've ever seen."

"I disagree," Japapa replied. "We know from what we discovered on the boat, the man's probably been dead for several days. The stench from his rotting body should overwhelm us but there's no odor. And nothing has begun to consume his body. Normally, land crabs would have torn away bits of his flesh and maggots would be crawling over his eyes and mouth. It appears whatever killed him killed everything else on this island, and I for one don't want to find out what it was. I suggest we return to the dinghy. We need to get the hell away from this place before something terrible happens to us."

As they headed away from the island, no one, including Japapa, took note of the tiny bubbles that were rising to the ocean's surface. Looking out across the bow of their vessel, Japapa pondered the death of the fisherman. Whatever was happening on that island was frightening. Perhaps it was a virus that had wiped out everything. If it was, hopefully neither he nor his men had contracted it. One thing was certain—he had no intention of ever returning to this place.

GARY SCHMELZ

CHAPTER

Somewhere Within the Bermuda Triangle

DECEMBER 2019

Someone was out there. Peering through a crack in the door, Wendell could sense them staring at him through the mist. What did they want? Sweat began to trickle down his forehead. It was getting harder for him to breathe. Stepping back from the door, he looked around for someplace to hide.

"Over here," an old woman's raspy voice beckoned.

Wendell turned. There was no one there. Again, the voice called out.

"Where are you?" Wendell gasped when the mist began to seep underneath the door.

"You must hurry," the voice warned. "The Chogers will soon be here."

"The Chogers? Who are the Chogers?" Wendell asked. *Taking another step backward, he stumbled over a chair.*

Before he could regain his balance, the mist surrounded him and a cold hand reached out and grabbed his slender arm. Unable to free himself, Wendell lunged forward and screamed.

"There's nothing to worry about," a friendly voice assured him.

Opening his eyes, Wendell sat back in his seat and realized he was having a nightmare.

"It's just a little air turbulence." The uniformed pilot smiled and turned towards Wendell in the copilot's seat. "Is this your first trip to the Bahamas?"

"Yeah," Wendell said, his brilliant smile generating a sharp contrast to his chocolate-colored skin. Rubbing the lids of his brown eyes, he ran his hand through his short, wiry, black hair, and tried to act nonchalantly. "I'm going to spend my Christmas break with my grandpa on Crooked Island," he offered. "My parents thought it would be good if I paid him a visit. They said he'd enjoy having me spend some time with him around the holidays. Normally, I'd be thrilled, but I'd made plans with my friends to do some ice skating in Central Park and then head up to Lake Placid to try some skiing."

Smiling, the blonde, curly-haired pilot guided the plane towards a narrow break in the clouds and checked his GPS reading. "It's too bad you'll miss out on skiing and skating, but I really think you'll enjoy spending your holiday on Crooked Island. It's one of my favorite places. What does your grandfather do?"

"He's a fisherman. Mom is always telling my sister and me stories about how she used to go fishing with him when she was little. She said they used to get lots of snapper and grouper. They also collected conch. She said they'd use the soft parts for bait and eat the foot."

"I really like raw conch. Have you ever tried it?" The stocky pilot glanced at the fuel gauges on the instrument panel of his twin engine Cessna Conquest.

"No. Grandpa brought some up to New York when he visited us a couple of months ago. Mom made a salad out of it. She wanted my sister and me to try it, but we thought it was disgusting. The idea of eating raw snail made me want to puke. Mom got mad when we wouldn't try it, but Grandpa just laughed. He said Mom acted the same way when he offered it to her the first time."

"Well, you should try it sometime." The plane entered another turbulent air pocket and began bouncing around. "Make sure your seat belt is tight," the pilot warned. "It looks like we're headed for some rough weather."

Wendell gave an extra tug at his belt and stared apprehensively at the massive storm clouds in front of them. Lightning lit up the billowing, grey clouds as large drops of rain pelted the windshield of the plane. This was his first flight in a small plane and it was a lot scarier than he expected.

"By the way, I failed to introduce myself when you got on board. My name is Travis." The pilot grinned and reached over to shake Wendell's hand.

"Do you make this trip often?" Wendell asked after shaking the pilot's hand and looking out of the side window of the plane.

"Yeah. I've been making it almost every other day for the last ten years. It's a real milk run. I think I could do it with my eyes shut. We usually have a full load of passengers in the winter, but the family of four that booked this flight cancelled because a close relative became seriously ill. Since you were going to be my only passenger, the company decided to fly some medical supplies to the Acklins. They're a series of islands just south of Crooked. Do you get to see your grandfather often?" Travis inquired before scanning his altimeter, air speed, and fuel gauges.

"Not as often as I'd like. If it had been at any other time, I'd really be excited about it. He's got a lot of great stories to tell. Once, he told my sister and me about a time when he and one of his friends went treasure hunting on the south end of Crooked. He said they discovered the ruins of some old houses that had been occupied by British Loyalists from the American Revolutionary War. According to Grandpa, these people brought a lot of gold and other treasures with them when they left the States. He said they would often bury it in secret places so pirates couldn't find it."

"Did they find anything?"

"Not a lot." Wendell sighed. "He said if there was anything, someone had gotten to the treasure before they did. But he did find one large gold coin. Grandpa showed it to me. He said he is going to give it to me on my eighteenth birthday."

"Wow, that's quite a find. What will you do with it?"

"I'm not sure. Maybe I'll sell it and use the money to help pay for college."

"That's smart. It's probably worth a lot of money." Travis guided the plane further to the southeast in order to avoid the cluster of approaching storms. "What do you think of the view? I thought you'd enjoy sitting in the copilot's seat. It's not too often a thirteen-year-old gets to sit up here."

"It's okay, I guess." Wendell peered nervously through the side window at a series of small islands that appeared through a break in the clouds.

"That's the south end of Great Exuma," Travis said. "I used to do some bone fishing there. We're flying at about 6,500 feet. Crooked Island and the Acklins are further south. We should be there in about forty minutes. There are about three thousand islands in the Bahamas. Grand Bahama Island and Great Abaco are the northernmost ones while Great Inagua is the furthest south. They say you can see Cuba from the lighthouse in Matthew Town in Inagua on a clear day. Most of these islands lie within what is called the Bermuda Triangle."

"What's the Bermuda Triangle?" Wendell asked as they passed through another turbulent pocket of air.

"It's a place where ships and airplanes have vanished under mysterious circumstances. According to the U. S. Navy, the triangle doesn't exist but a lot of people disagree. They say that too many unexplained disappearances have occurred in this region for it not to be real. Some folks attribute the disappearance of ships and planes to alien life forms."

Thinking about his recent nightmare, Wendell turned towards the pilot and asked him what he thought about the Bermuda Triangle.

"The whole idea of the Triangle and alien life forms sounds far-fetched to me. I wouldn't take anything you hear about the Triangle too seriously. I think it's a lot of nonsense writers make up to sell books."

Another bright flash of lightning caught Wendell's attention. "Thunderstorms always crop up around this time of year when cold fronts move through," Travis said. "Most of the time I can avoid them, but it looks like I'll have to fly through this one. Hang on. It's going to get really rough."

Noticing his main fuel tanks were nearly empty, Travis switched to his auxiliary supply and attempted to find a less turbulent route through the storm. His visibility was next to nothing and every few seconds a bolt of lightning enveloped the plane in a blinding flash of white light. Neither the pilot nor Wendell were prepared for what came next. Without warning, the plane was flung sideways by a pocket of severe turbulence and its engines began to sputter and shake violently.

A wide-eyed Wendell grabbed hold of his seat and shouted to Travis, "What's happening!?"

"I don't know," the pilot frowned. "There are no warning lights showing up on the instrument panel."

"What about that one?" Wendell asked anxiously and pointed to a small light on the panel.

"That's the emergency locator beacon," Travis shouted as the violent shaking continued. "It's set to go off automatically whenever the plane goes through severe turbulence. From the sound of the engines, it looks like I might have picked up some bad fuel."

"C-can we make it to Crooked Island?" a terrified Wendell stammered while looking out the window hoping to catch sight of land.

"I'm certain we can," Travis assured him. As the pilot continued to monitor his instruments, Wendell's anxiety mounted.

All at once, the violent shaking ceased and the Cessna's two engines stopped running. For a brief moment, both the pilot and Wendell sat in stunned silence as the plane started a nosedive towards the ocean. Instinctively, Travis picked up the radio transmitter and began shouting "MAYDAY!" while the knot in Wendell's stomach and the sour taste in his mouth let him know that the Dunkin' Donuts he had devoured for breakfast were about to reappear. Within seconds the plane plummeted 2,000 feet. Then another bolt of lightning lit up the sky and Travis spotted a small island directly in front of them.

"Quick, unlatch the side door at the rear of the plane and jam it open with your backpack," Travis shouted while he tried to level off the plane and restart the engines. From that moment, everything Wendell did seemed to be in slow motion—except for the donuts which erupted all over the plane's instrument panel.

"Hurry up! We don't have much time!" Travis screamed as the plane started to level off. Unbuckling his seat belt Wendell scrambled to the back of the plane and struggled to open the door's handle.

"The handle's stuck," Wendell shouted back. "I can't get it open."

"You must! I'm going to ditch the plane close to that island we just passed over. When we hit the water the plane might flip over. If that happens it's important that the door is open so the cabin can fill with water and we can get out. After you finish jamming the door open, get back up front. Your life jacket is under the seat. Put it on but don't inflate it. Then buckle up, place your head down against your knees and hold on to your seat for dear life."

One last shove and the door gave way. Reaching for his backpack, Wendell jammed it between the open door and the frame of the plane.

"The door's jammed open," Wendell yelled while struggling to get back to his seat. "Is there anything else you want me to do?"

"No!" Travis shouted. "Just strap yourself in and prepare for a crash landing."

After reaching the front of the plane, Wendell pulled out the life jacket, put it on, tightened his seatbelt, and grabbed hold of his seat.

"Pray!" were the last words he heard Travis say before they slammed into the turbulent ocean.

CHAPTER

Landrail, Crooked Island, Bahamas

DECEMBER 2019

As Reggie wept over the wooden caskets of his mother and father, he recalled the accident in Nassau. There was a blood spattered, cracked windshield in the rental car and someone shouting, "Call for an ambulance. I think dey are dead."

"What about de boy?" someone else cried out in anguish.

Next, he'd felt the stubby fingers of a man reaching through the car window and feeling for his pulse.

"He's alive," the man had answered with relief.

Sirens wailed in the distance. A woman bent over and whispered words of encouragement. "Help is on de way," she sobbed as tears ran down her plump cheeks. "Try ta hang on."

He hated the man who rammed his truck into them. The police said he was a drunk who had lost control of his vehicle.

He deserved to be in prison Reggie thought, *but the authorities had let him go. There were rumors it was because he came from a wealthy family with political connections. Why should that matter?*

The day of the accident had begun with such promise. His father had announced he finally had the money to buy some land on Fortune Island where he planned to build a home. They'd been headed to the bank in Nassau to complete the transaction. It had taken his parents years to earn the money to buy the property, and then, in one terrible instant, their entire world had been shattered.

A gentle hand reached out and squeezed Reggie's shoulder. "It's time ta go," his Uncle Lewis said with tear-filled eyes.

Stepping back from the coffins, they watched the pallbearers hoist the plainly constructed mahogany boxes and head towards the tiny church graveyard. It hadn't rained in weeks, and the swirling wind generated by an approaching cold front dusted the grieving relatives' dark suits with a thin veneer of limestone dust as they trudged to the top of the hill. Two shallow graves laboriously carved from the rocky soil greeted them at the burial site. In the distance, ominous purple clouds gathered near the horizon and a loud roll of thunder briefly interrupted the preacher as he began the graveside service.

Reggie never heard the words that followed. With pursed lips, he kept thinking about an argument he'd had with his uncle the day before. His uncle was insisting that Reggie move to Nassau to live with one of his other relatives, but Reggie had pleaded with him to let him stay on Crooked Island. The argument had ended with neither side giving in, but Reggie knew the decision about his future had been sealed. Suddenly, the preacher stopped talking and everyone's eyes turned towards Reggie. Stepping forward, Reggie lifted a shovelful of rocky soil and tossed it on his parents' coffins. As he did, the sobs of grieving relatives grew louder and renewed anger and frustration welled up inside him. *It just wasn't right*, Reggie thought as he stepped back from the grave and watched his uncle and several of the local residents finish covering the coffins.

That afternoon, when all his relatives had left, Reggie sat across the table from Uncle Lewis and stared at his grieving relative in silence. His mother's portly brother was cradling his round face in his scarred hands and staring at the white tablecloth in front of him. After several moments of painful silence, he lowered his hands and lifted his head. Outside, a torrential rain shower drowned out the complaints of the family's goats as he began to speak. "I've gotten you a plane ticket fer Nassau," he began hesitatingly. "It leaves tomorrow at noon."

How come he wasn't surprised by dat decision, Reggie thought as he continued to stare at his uncle. After a brief pause, he wiped the tears from his cheeks and announced he wasn't going.

"Please be reasonable, Reggie," his uncle pleaded. "You need a proper home. Your mother and father were only living with us until dey got enough money ta build der own house. Your dad never took out a life insurance policy, and de man dat caused de accident disappeared after he was released on bail. Dos rumors about him coming from a rich family and having political connections weren't true. De money your folks had ta buy de property went fer de funeral. Dat means der isn't any money ta take care of you. Heaven knows, we'd love ta have you stay with us, but we can't afford another mouth ta feed. Your aunt and uncle in Nassau have a big home and dey'd love ta have you."

"I can take care of myself." Reggie lifted his slender body from the table and stomped across the room to the kitchen window. Huge droplets of rain pelted the glass, and Reggie stared at the reflection of his tormented black face and bloodshot eyes. "My dad taught me how ta fish. I can earn enough money ta make a living doing dat!"

"And what about school?" Uncle Lewis asked. "Your mother and father made me promise dat if anything ever happened ta dem, I'd see ta it dat you completed your education."

"I'm fourteen years old. I don't need any more schoolin'," Reggie said as tears welled up in the corners of his eyes. With pursed lips, he watched the dust-filled raindrops cascading down the windowpane. "Schoolin' isn't going ta make me a better fisherman. Some of de best fishermen on Crooked Island have never finished school," he sobbed.

"Well, a promise is a promise," Uncle Lewis sighed. "Your mother and father would never have approved of dat. Dey wanted you ta have a better life dan dey did. I'm sorry about what's happened. I miss your parents just as much as you do, and I wish der was some way I could bring dem back. But what's done is done, and der ain't no way any of us is going ta undo dat terrible car accident."

"I don't care about your promise!" Reggie shouted. Before his uncle could respond, Reggie bolted out of the house into the swirling rain. Stumbling to the front door, Lewis spotted his nephew silhouetted by a flash of lightning. He was racing towards the ocean engulfed in a billowing accumulation of black clouds.

It wasn't until early evening that Reggie's uncle found his nephew miles from his house, sitting on the edge of a lime rock cliff and staring out across the storm swept ocean. When he asked him to come home, Reggie nodded without saying a word and followed him slowly back to the house.

Tomorrow, things will be different, Reggie thought to himself as the roar of the surf faded into the distance. *Tomorrow, I will show everyone what kind of man I am.*

CHAPTER

Port-au-Prince, Haiti

DECEMBER 2019

"It's time to leave." An anxious Claude Joseph looked over at his daughter, Simone, and smiled. She was a bright and beautiful young girl. Like the rest of her family, she was fluent in both English and French and had achieved very good grades at the private school she attended. At thirteen, it wouldn't be long before admiring young men would come knocking at his door to ask permission to take her on a date. Her long, black hair glistened when she brushed it away from the side of her face and the smile that greeted you was bound to melt the heart of any young suitor. However, his daughter's future and that of the rest of his family were in grave danger. If they had any chance of surviving, they must leave Haiti and escape to the United States. He had a brother living in Miami. Once they arrived, they could live with him and seek asylum. They would be safe there, and he could provide Simone and her younger brother with a more secure and promising life.

Motioning for his daughter to hurry, Claude sighed. "We must leave Port-au-Prince tonight. Our boat is scheduled to depart tomorrow at sunset."

"I don't see why we have to go," a dejected Simone grumbled as she stuffed some of her most precious possessions into a small satchel. "Why can't we hide in the mountains like everyone else until it's safe to return home?"

Handing Simone the last few items she had lying on top of her dresser, Claude placed his hand on his daughter's shoulder and gave her a sympathetic look. "We've gone over this before. It's too dangerous for us to remain on the island. Former members of the country's secret police have been watching us for days. They've been abducting and murdering everyone they think is a threat to them. Our government is once again in a state of chaos. The office of the new president, Javenal Moise, is under siege by these thugs and there are rumors that Japapa, an old enemy of mine, is attempting to return to Haiti to take control of the government. Just yesterday, his followers killed my best friend, Adrian, and in a day or two they may decide to do the same to me. They don't trust the staff at the university and they're well aware of the role I played in overthrowing the previous regime."

"I guess you're right," a dejected Simone replied as they left the bedroom, "but I'd feel a lot better if I weren't having nightmares. I can't get those images of that young mother and her child out of my mind. And that wretched old woman in the cave terrifies me."

"I don't know what your dreams signify," a concerned Claude responded as they headed towards the kitchen. "Hopefully nothing. I only know it's even more dangerous for us to remain here in Haiti."

Simone pouted and thought about leaving all her school friends. "It's just not fair. How long will it be before we are able to come back?"

"I don't know," her father said. He stepped to the window and looked out onto the dark street. "We'll just have to wait and see how things turn out. If my old enemy, Japapa, gains control of the country, we'll never be able to return. Our people will remain poor and there will be more abductions and killings. I can only pray to God that he's not successful and that things will turn out differently. If they do, we will be the first to come back—I promise you. But for now, it will be better for us to stay with your uncle in the States."

As Simone's father kept a watchful eye on the street, he caught sight of a man stepping out of the alleyway and heading towards their home. "Turn out the lights and be quiet," he warned. "Someone's coming."

A moment later the man rapped on the door and demanded to know if this was the home of Claude Joseph.

CHAPTER

Open Water South of French Wells, Crooked Island

DECEMBER 2019

Water began pouring into the plane as soon as it hit the ocean and flipped over.

Releasing his seat belt, Wendell fell to the roof of the cabin and turned around to look for Travis. Blood was running down the pilot's face and his left arm and leg were severely twisted.

"Pull out the inflatable life raft. It's in the back of the plane," Travis yelled. Trying to forget the pain coursing through his body, he struggled to free himself. "Hurry! We don't have much time," he moaned.

Turning around, Wendell spotted the raft, released it from its compartment on the cabin floor, and began pulling it towards the door. Somehow, Travis managed to arrive first. Straining, he pushed the door open further and passed the backpack to Wendell. The water in the cabin was turning crimson from the blood seeping out of the pilot's wounds and Wendell was beginning to wonder if Travis would survive.

"Push the raft outside and inflate it," Travis said, his face contorted with pain. "Just yank on the cord. I'll be right behind you."

Squirming through the opening, Wendell scrambled into the inflated raft and yanked his life vest cord. The rain and waves made it almost impossible to see as the raft drifted away from the wreckage. Anxiously looking around, Wendell shouted to the pilot, "Over here!" But there was no response.

The plane had nearly disappeared beneath the waves and there was still no sign of Travis. Wendell shouted again. Still no response. Panic started to set in. Shielding his eyes from the torrential downpour, Wendell continued looking for the injured pilot. It was no use; he couldn't see a thing. Then Travis's grimacing face bobbed above the surface. Grabbing hold of the raft's safety line, the exhausted pilot implored Wendell to pull him on board.

Reaching over the side, Wendell took hold of Travis's good arm and belt and pulled. Agonizing screams followed. Travis's weight and his inability to generate a lot of forward momentum made it impossible for Wendell to drag him into the raft.

"I can't do it," Wendell groaned.

"You must," Travis pleaded. "I can't be left out here alone. I'll die."

Leaning over, Wendell tried again. It was still no use. He didn't have enough strength to hoist him into the raft and the pilot was too weak to provide any assistance. In need of another solution, Wendell looked around. The rain had begun to subside and he was able to make out the fuzzy outline of an island in the distance.

"Land!" Wendell shouted and pointed. "I think it's the island we spotted from the air."

"How far away?" Travis moaned.

"Not far. I think we can make it. The storm appears to be moving away from us."

"Good," Travis gasped. "There're some oars in the raft. See if you can paddle towards it."

Nothing went as Wendell hoped. It seemed to take an eternity to find the oars and he had a terrible time trying to paddle against the wind. Meanwhile, Travis was growing weaker. Fortunately for Wendell, the current was working in their favor. *We might just make it*, he thought to himself when Travis screamed, "SHARKS!"

A minute ago, there was nothing. Now there were six huge fins circling the raft.

"How much further?" Travis shouted as the hungry creatures moved closer.

"Maybe a quarter of a mile," Wendell yelled, panicked by the terror etched on the pilot's face, his pleading eyes begging for help.

"It's too far," Travis shouted "You've got to get me out of the water. They smell my blood."

Dropping the oars, Wendell lunged over the side and began pulling the pilot into the raft. This time, with Travis's help, it seemed to be working.

"Just a little bit more," Wendell grunted, "and you'll be safe."

"Oh God!" Travis cried. The force of the shark's attack jolted the pilot backwards and pulled him free of Wendell's grip. There were no further screams, only the twisting gyrations of the shark tearing into the pilot's body.

Sliding back from the edge of the raft, Wendell watched the onslaught with horrified disbelief. When it was over, Travis's right arm was all that remained attached to the safety line. Traumatized and frozen with fear, Wendell was suddenly knocked on his back and his backpack hurled into the water. A shark was attempting to toss him overboard. Fearing for his life, he grabbed one of the oars and frantically resumed paddling towards the island. As he looked into the storm tossed water, one of the beasts turned on its side and eyed him from below. It was a bloodthirsty look he'd never forget.

CHAPTER

Landrail, Crooked Island

Finally, everyone appeared to be asleep. Quietly slipping out of his bed, Reggie listened once more to make sure his uncle and the rest of his family had not heard him get up. When no one stirred, he stepped out the front door and followed the moonlit path that led to the beach. A stiff, northwesterly breeze was blowing, and the sweet fragrance of honeysuckle filled the refreshing, cool night air.

Barefoot in the turbulent surf, with his sneakers tied around his neck, Reggie waded out to his boat and hoisted his gear aboard the single-mast dinghy. The fourteen-foot sailboat was his prize possession. His dad had helped him build it more than a year ago for his thirteenth birthday. Together they'd collected wood from one of the nearby islands and hauled it back to the house, where his father introduced him to the skills of boat building. The ribs, stem and sternposts were made from

Bahamian dogwood and horseflesh trees, while the keel and outer planks were made from hard island pine. It had taken them months to apply the finishing touches but the hard work paid off. The *Sea Star* turned out to be a rugged little craft, well-suited for traveling across the shallow, reef-filled waters surrounding Crooked Island.

After pulling himself aboard, Reggie carefully checked to make sure the tent, cooking utensils, and other supplies he had stowed away earlier were still there. Satisfied he had everything he needed, he pulled up the anchor and unfurled the sail. Both the tide and the wind were in his favor. The boat swiftly headed south as the morning sun began to peek above the billowing purple storm clouds that were drifting southeast towards the horizon.

Fortune Island was his destination. He and his father had visited the place a couple of times when they went fishing for lobster and conch. His father had discovered an abandoned house near the south end and had taken Reggie to see it. The house was situated on a hill just above one of the most beautiful palm fringed beaches he'd ever seen. He hoped someday their family could live there, but a drunk driver had put an end to that dream. Now, Reggie was determined to make his father's vision a reality. He would return to the abandoned house and move into it. Using driftwood that washed ashore, he'd make the necessary repairs and then earn a living fishing for lobster and conch.

The water was taking on the golden glow of the rising sun as the storm clouds drifted beyond the horizon. Reggie could sense this beautiful island beckoning. It was as if some magical force was drawing him towards it. His spirits soared with thoughts of his new life and how proud his father would be. Glancing briefly at his compass to confirm his heading, he made a minor correction to the *Sea Star*'s course and sat back to enjoy the ride. A small pod of playful bottlenose dolphins surfaced near the bow and raced ahead as if guiding him to his new home. Everything was going according to plan when a flash of lightning streaked across the sky and the dolphins vanished. A second line of thunderstorms was approaching from the northwest. Realizing he was about to be engulfed by severe weather, Reggie began looking for shelter. Goat Cay offered the nearest safe harbor. He adjusted his sail into the cutting edge of the wind, enabling the craft to skim across the turbulent waters towards the tiny island. It was a close race. The swiftly moving line of storms nearly caught up with him before he was able to maneuver into the island's protected lagoon. Once inside, Reggie breathed a sigh of relief and watched with awe as large, wind-driven waves pounded the cove's jagged lime rock entrance.

Behind the blanket of grey clouds, a cooler northwesterly breeze swept across the island. Closer to shore, he threw out his anchor and waded to the beach with his drybag slung over his shoulder. Shivering beneath the shelter of some palm trees, Reggie put on his jacket and dry clothes. Next, he needed to find some wood to start a fire. Winter storms often tossed a lot of driftwood onto the island beaches but most of what he initially found was too wet. Pulling the collar of his jacket up around his neck, he headed further inland. There, he found enough dry brush to start a fire under the shelter of some trees.

The backside of the dunes, near where he anchored his boat, seemed like the best place to set up camp. After hauling several piles of brush to the temporary site, Reggie grabbed some matches from his bag and ignited the wood. It took a while for the flames to generate enough warmth. Huddling close to the fire, he rubbed his hands together and waited for the heat to drive the chill out of his body.

Once he warmed up, his stomach started to complain about a lack of food. Moving to the top of the dune, he surveyed the exposed flats for pink conch. These beautiful snails, with their flaring pink lips, were a favorite among the tourists who loved to decorate their homes with the empty shells. For Reggie, they were an easy source of nourishment. Walking to an exposed sandbar, he picked up several mature animals and piled them on the beach. Next, he began scanning the rocky shoreline looking for a nearshore reef where he could spear some fish, but after checking out the shallow waters of the lagoon, he decided the water was too murky and rough for that. It was then he noticed a bright orange object washed up on a stretch of jagged lime rock beach. Excited by the prospect it might be something useful, he made his way along the rugged shoreline to take a closer look. Perhaps, it was a crate of fruit washed overboard from a cargo ship or better yet a buoy. As it turned out, it was neither. Wedged between the rocks he found an empty, blood-spattered raft, with a fly-covered human arm twisted in its safety line.

CHAPTER

Home of Claude Joseph, Port-au-Prince, Haiti

"We must leave now," an impatient voice from behind the door implored. "I'm Michel Francois. I've been sent to take you to the ship."

Letting out a sigh of relief, Claude Joseph unlatched the door and cautiously permitted the weathered old man into the house. "Some people are watching you very closely," Michel whispered. "I have diverted their attention, but they'll be back. Are you ready?"

"Yes," a nervous Claude Joseph responded. "Were you able to find some gasoline?"

"*Wi*," the man responded in Creole, "but it cost me a lot more than I anticipated. Everyone wants it."

Reaching into his back pocket, Claude pulled out his wallet and offered Michel an additional hundred dollars in American currency. "Will that be enough?"

"*Wi*, but we must hurry," an anxious Michel whispered. "I've parked the car several blocks away. I didn't want your neighbors to see me drive up to your house. Leave a light on when you depart. That way the people who were watching will believe you're still here when they return."

"Right." Claude turned on the kitchen light and waited for his family to step out onto the street. Simone and her younger brother, Michael, were the first to join Michel followed by Claude and his wife Marie.

"This way," Michel whispered and motioned with his slender arm for them to follow. Hearts pounding, they moved cautiously down the dark, rancid smelling street with its narrow, broken sidewalks. The night air was humid, and the least amount of noise caused them to stop and hold their breath. Rats scurried from piles of uncollected garbage, and the voices of homeless people drifted from blind alleyways.

The car was parked on an unlit street. A few frantic moments passed after they turned on the ignition and looked around to see if anyone was listening. As far as they could tell no one was. Sighs of relief were followed by the repeated knocks of the car's tired engine. Down each rubble-lined street and bend in the road they suspected people were watching. *Will they report us?* Claude thought as he spotted several shadowy figures disappear through narrow doorways into unlit houses—hopefully not.

CHAPTER

Wendell's Family's Apartment, New York City

"How was the zoo?" Ben Jenkins asked his daughter, Amy, who was skipping down the apartment hallway to greet him.

"It was really neat." Amy threw her slender brown arms around her father and gave him a kiss. "I think my favorite animals were the panda and the reticulated giraffes. I hope I can go back real soon."

"We'll see," Ben replied as he removed his reading glasses and returned his daughter's embrace. "Did Mom have fun too?"

"I guess, but she didn't like the snakes. She said they were yucky and gave her the creeps."

"They were yucky," Emily Jenkins interjected. Walking across the living room still wearing her red, winter coat, she gave her husband a big kiss. "I've always hated those things. I can still remember one of them slithering into our yard on Crooked Island and swallowing one of our chickens."

"You can't blame it for that," Ben teased, returning his wife's kiss. "It was hungry."

"We were hungry, too," Emily snapped back while removing her coat and hanging it in the closet, "and every time one of them ate a chicken, the hens would stop laying for a week. Not to change the subject, but has my father called about Wendell?" Emily asked brushing her long, black hair away from her face.

"No, not yet," Ben responded. "I know it's a little late, but your cousin in Fort Lauderdale said that the plane didn't take off until 1:00. I'm sure your father will call the minute Wendell gets there."

"I suppose, but I'd certainly feel a lot better knowing he's made it safely."

"I wish I'd gone with Wendell," Amy interrupted. "I like being with Grandpa. It would have been neat to listen to his stories and spend some time fishing."

"Maybe when you're a little older," Emily said, playfully tousling her daughter's curly hair. "But now it's time to wash up and get ready for dinner. I've made something special."

"All right." Amy raced gleefully towards the bathroom. "I hope it's chocolate-covered brownies."

Shaking her head, an amused smile spread across Emily's face. She put her arm around her husband's slender waist and guided him towards the kitchen. "And what have you been doing with yourself while we've been gone?" Emily asked as Ben's new iPhone began to ring.

"Not much. I finished paying some bills and did a little office work." Reaching over, he picked up the phone hoping it wasn't someone trying to sell him something. "Hello."

"Is this the Jenkins' residence?" a person inquired.

"Yes," Ben responded warily.

"Sir, my name is Brad Connors. I'm with Trans-Bahamas Airways in Fort Lauderdale. I believe your son, Wendell, was traveling on one of our charter planes to Crooked Island?"

"Yes. Why? Is there a problem?"

"I'm afraid there is," Brad replied and paused. "We just received word that the plane your son was flying on crashed somewhere near Crooked Island."

"Is he ok?" Ben asked as he felt the blood rush from his face and his legs go limp.

"I regret to say we don't know yet. Our initial report is sketchy. A search plane has been dispatched to see if they can spot anything. When they report back, we'll give you a call."

Ben looked over at his wife with tear-filled eyes and asked, "Is there anything we can do?"

"I'm afraid not. All any of us can do right now is sit tight and wait for the reconnaissance plane to report back."

"How long before you'll know something?" Ben inquired. Anticipating bad news, Emily raised her hand to her mouth and stared at her husband with wide-eyed disbelief.

"Several hours at least—maybe not until tomorrow. The weather is bad and they don't have much daylight to work with."

"Please let us know the minute you learn anything."

"I promise—I'm sorry to be the bearer of such bad news. If I can help you in any way please let me know."

"We will," Ben said numbly and he hung up the phone. Emily continued to stare at her husband, dreading to hear what he had to say. "It's about Wendell," Ben said softly. "His plane went down near Crooked Island. They've sent out a search plane to look for him."

Stunned by the news, Emily collapsed into the kitchen chair and began to cry.

CHAPTER

Goat Cay, South of French Wells, Bahamas

A soft moan arose from behind the raft. Cautiously making his way across the rugged limestone shoreline, Reggie spotted Wendell lying face down in a weathered depression. His body was covered with blood with one of his arms awkwardly folded underneath his chest.

"Mon, are you all right?" Reggie asked. Kneeling, he gently placed his hand on Wendell's back.

"S-sharks," Wendell mumbled as he tried to get up. "We've got to get away from them."

"Der are no sharks here. You've been washed ashore on Goat Cay."

"They got Travis," Wendell sobbed. "I couldn't save him."

"Who's Travis? A friend?"

"No, he was the pilot," Wendell said as he mustered up enough strength to roll onto his side, tears running down his cheeks. "We were flying to Crooked Island. Something happened to the plane's engines and we crashed."

"Was anyone else with you?"

"No."

"Well, you can't stay here," Reggie said and looked for a way to drag Wendell away from the rocks. "De tide will come in and fill dis hole with water. Do you think you have any broken bones?"

"I don't think so," Wendell said, slowly moving his arms and legs before he sat up. "But I hurt all over."

"I believe dat. You're pretty banged up, Mon. If I give you my hand, do you think you can lift yourself up so I can get you out of here?"

"I'll try, but I don't feel so good."

"I'm not surprised," Reggie said as he leaned over to offer Wendell some support. "Try ta reach over and put your arm around my neck."

"Ok," Wendell sighed as he made a feeble attempt to get up.

"Do you have a good grip?" Reggie asked.

"Yeah, but I think I'm going to be sick," Wendell groaned as Reggie began to lift him.

"Try ta hold on 'til I get you away from here."

"I can't." Wendell gagged and spewed out a bellyful of seawater.

"Feel any better?" Reggie asked after giving Wendell a few moments to recuperate.

"I've felt better," Wendell gasped. Using his free hand, he wiped away the vomit running down his chin.

"Let's get across dese rocks," Reggie urged. "You'll be a lot more comfortable once you sit down on de beach."

Wendell thought he'd never make it. His body shook from the cold and several times his knees buckled causing Reggie to stop so he could lift him up. "We're almost der," Reggie grunted when they reached the edge of a large sand dune. "Just a few more steps and you can sit down."

The remaining steps up the dune were sheer agony, and when they got to the top, Wendell collapsed onto his back, too exhausted to move.

"Now dat we're here, I'll clean up dos cuts," Reggie said. Removing the tattered remains of Wendell's shirt, he shook the sand out of it and shouted above the wind, "I'll be back in a minute. I need ta rinse your shirt so I can clean your wounds."

At the water's edge, Reggie began to think about the young man he'd just rescued. *The raft is a real problem,* he thought as he soaked the boy's bloody shirt. *It's something I'll have ta deal with later. Right now, I need ta see what I can do fer de boy.*

"Can you sit up?" Reggie asked when he returned. "I need ta look at de wounds on your back."

"All right," Wendell sighed.

Examining Wendell's back, Reggie grimaced. "Mon, you've got some deep cuts. I'm going ta use your shirt ta clean dem out so dey don't get infected. Dis is going ta sting."

"Ouch!" Wendell winced when Reggie wiped away some dirt from one of the deeper cuts. "Do you have to rub so hard?"

"I'm trying not ta, Mon, but I've got ta make sure dat des cuts don't get any worse. If dey do, you'll regret it. Was der a first aid kit on de raft?"

"I don't know," Wendell moaned. "Maybe."

"Let me check it out." Standing up, Reggie turned to see if the raft had floated out with the incoming tide and gave a sigh of relief when he saw it drifting near the water's edge. "It'll only take me a minute ta see if it's der."

After running down to retrieve the kit, Reggie pulled the raft further up the beach and made a mental note of how he would dispose of it. "You're lucky," Reggie said when he returned and started applying an antibiotic salve to Wendell's face, arms, and back. "De kit was still on de raft. Dis will burn, but it'll feel a lot better after I put it on your cuts."

When Reggie finished, he stepped back and grinned. "I believe I did a pretty good job if I do say so myself. Can you make it further down de beach?"

"I guess," Wendell groaned.

"Good. Lean on me. I'll get you set up next ta de fire I've started. I've got some dry clothes you can try on. Dey'll help keep you warm. It's going ta get chilly tonight. Meanwhile, I'll get some water from my boat and hunt up some food."

"All right," Wendell moaned. Grabbing hold of Reggie's arm, he grimaced in pain as he pulled himself up. "I don't think I've introduced myself. My name's Wendell—Wendell Jenkins."

"Pleased ta meet you, Wendell," Reggie said with a big toothy grin. "I'm Reggie Sands."

"Well, I'm certainly glad to meet you, Reggie. I don't know what would have happened if you hadn't come along."

Neither do I, Reggie thought to himself as they trudged down the beach.

…

CHAPTER

Harbor Docks, Port-au-Prince, Haiti

"I'll need two thousand more in cash," the bearded Bahamian boat captain demanded after counting Claude Joseph's money.

"But that's not what we agreed upon," Claude argued. Shaking his head in disgust, he stared at the man's shifty eyes. "You quoted me three thousand a person!"

"I know. But dat was before de United States increased de number of patrol boats. If dey catch me doing dis I could lose my vessel."

"I understand—but a bargain is a bargain," Claude grumbled, "I don't have any more money. I've used up everything I had to pay for this trip."

"I hear de same story from nearly everyone." The captain's scarred face elicited a contemptuous grin. "But I have ta watch out fer myself. If you can't pay me den der are lots of others who can. See dat group of people standing over der? Every one of dem is willing ta pay me what I want."

Claude didn't know if the boat captain was bluffing, but he couldn't risk losing his family's only hope of reaching the United States. "Will you take something besides cash?" he asked.

"I might. Depends on what you have."

"I have a gold watch, and my wife has some jewelry that's been in her family for generations."

The captain stroked his bearded chin and pondered Claude Joseph's offer. "Show me," he said with a glimmer of interest. Opening a suitcase that contained the family's prized possessions, Claude pulled out a small metal box and unlocked it so the captain could inspect its contents. Initially, he seemed pleased as he eagerly fondled each piece of jewelry. Then the captain frowned and asked, "Is dis all you have?"

Stunned, Claude clenched his fists and glared into the greedy man's eyes. A surge of anger raced through his body. Under different circumstances, he would have struck the man but that wouldn't have done him any good. "Yes," he responded after getting his temper under control, "and it's worth twice as much as you're asking."

"Perhaps," the captain grinned, "but I don't always get as much money fer jewelry as you might think. I tell you what, you give me de watch and de jewelry and we'll call it even."

"That's highway robbery!" Claude shouted.

"Take it or leave it," the captain shrugged. "We don't have much time. Der are lots of other families waiting ta take your place."

"You don't give me much choice," a furious Claude grumbled before handing over his watch and the jewelry and motioning to his wife and children to follow him aboard the rusted hulk of the cargo ship.

After climbing up the gangway and into the bowels of the ship, the Josephs found themselves crammed together in a suffocating cargo hold with dozens of other desperate people. The smell of sweat and remains of rotting food filled the compartment with a horrible stench, and Claude knew that one nightmare was about to be replaced by another.

CHAPTER

Goat Cay

When Wendell awoke from his short nap, he was greeted by the delicious scent of fresh meat being cooked over an open fire and his stomach started growling. "That smells great." Rolling over, he yawned and stretched his arms. Staring at the fire, his hunger pangs quickly subsided when he realized he was looking at the charred remains of two large lizards. "Iguanas," Reggie smiled proudly. "Dis island is full of dem. After you fell asleep, I hunted dem down."

"Yuck. I can't eat that," Wendell grumbled. "They're disgusting."

"Dey are really good, Mon." Reggie smiled and removed the lizards from the fire. Tearing off a round leaf from a sea grape tree, he placed one of the animal's tails on it and offered it to Wendell. "Dey taste better dan chicken."

"Well, I refuse to eat it. It's gross."

"Come on, Mon, try some," Reggie urged. "De tail is de best part. It's delicious. Just make sure dat you remove de skin first."

"Take it away." Wendell grimaced as he shoved aside Reggie's offering. "Couldn't you find something less disgusting to eat? Where's the water you said you were getting from your boat?"

"Right here. Try not ta gulp down ta much all at once. It'll make you sick. Besides, it's all I've got until I collect some coconuts."

"All right," Wendell said as he sipped from the jug.

"I did find some conch if you don't want de lizards. I could pull one of dem out of de shell and cut it up into small pieces. Dey are pretty good. Some of de tourists dat visit de Bahamas love ta eat dem raw."

"No way. That's almost as disgusting as the lizard. How about some fish or fruit?"

"It was ta rough fer me ta head out and spear fish." Reggie reached over and picked up his pack, "But I do have some mangoes."

"What are they?"

"Fruit," Reggie replied. "Dey came from a tree in my uncle's backyard. Here, take one. Dey are sweet."

Reaching across, Wendell took the yellowish green fruit and examined it carefully. "What's that smell?" Wendell asked as he lifted the mango up to his nose and scrunched his face. "It smells like the stuff my dad uses to clean his paint brushes."

"I don't know. It smells all right ta me," Reggie chuckled before devouring the leg and tail meat of one of the iguanas.

"Here, use my knife ta peel de skin off before you eat it. Some people get a rash from de skin."

After stripping the skin away, Wendell carefully reexamined the fruit before licking its juicy flesh.

"Mon, I've never seen such a fussy eater." An amused Reggie shook his head and watched Wendell cautiously bite into the mango. "How does it taste?"

"Not bad," Wendell said after taking several more mouthfuls. "You're right; it is pretty sweet."

"Well, I hope it suits your majesty's appetite," Reggie said sarcastically and pulled the last bit of meat away from the iguana's tail before tossing the bones underneath a sea grape tree. "It's all I've got ta offer you 'til tomorrow."

"It'll do," Wendell replied as he continued to devour the rest of the succulent fruit.

"Tomorrow, I'll spear some fish," Reggie said as he watched Wendell finish the first mango and ask for more. Reaching into his backpack, he pulled out another large, ripe fruit and smiled. "Are you sure you don't want some iguana?"

"I'm certain," Wendell grumbled. Grabbing the second mango from Reggie's hand, he quickly began to peel it and gobble it down.

"I'm glad you're feeling better," Reggie responded as he tore the head off another iguana and began to eat. "Why were you going ta Crooked Island?"

"To spend the Christmas break with my grandpa," Wendell said as he used the back of his hand to wipe away the mango juice running down his chin. "He's a fisherman. He was born on the island."

"What's his name?" Reggie asked after finishing the rest of the iguana. "I know most of de fisherman dat live der."

"Wilson Cooper," Wendell said while looking for a place to clean his sticky hands. "He's my grandfather on my mother's side. Mom was born and raised on Crooked Island."

"Mon, I know old man Cooper," Reggie said as he searched for his pot to fill with seawater. "He's one of de best fisherman on de island. My father learned a lot from him. I remember visiting his house a couple of times when my dad was alive. Dey talked about fishing all de time. I bet my father even knew your mom."

"Her name is Emily," Wendell added excitedly.

"Emily . . . it seems ta me I remember my mom and dad mentioning her. How long ago did she live here?"

"About twenty-five years ago. She finished high school and moved to Nassau to find a job. That's where she met my dad. They both moved to the States and went to college. My dad became a doctor and my mom's a schoolteacher."

"Did your mom have a dog called Bones?"

"Yeah. He used to follow her to school all the time. One Halloween she said she and her friends dressed him up as a goblin and went trick or treating. Apparently, he scared the wits out of all the young kids."

"Well, I'll be." Reggie shook his head in amazement. "I'm sure my folks knew her. In fact, I think dey even helped dress up her dog."

"Geez, that's hard to believe. Here I am in the middle of nowhere and I meet somebody whose family knew my mom. What a small world. Do your folks still live on Crooked?"

For a moment, Reggie remained silent and stared out over the water. When he turned to answer Wendell's question, tears had begun to form in the corners of his eyes.

"My mom and dad both died in a car accident a couple weeks ago." Reggie sobbed and began to wash his hands in the pot of seawater. "It happened in Nassau. A truck ran into de car we were in."

"Gosh, that's tough," Wendell said as he began to think about his own brush with death and the fact that his mother and father must be worried sick about him. "Are you living with relatives?"

"No," Reggie replied brusquely and wiped away the tears running down his cheeks. "I don't need any relatives. I can take care of myself."

"What are you going to do now that they're gone?" Wendell asked.

"Find a place ta live and start ta earn a living as a fisherman. I learned a lot about fishing from my dad."

"Well, I certainly wouldn't want to be in your shoes," Wendell said as thoughts about being rescued entered his mind. "How long do you think it'll be before someone comes out to rescue me?"

"I don't know. Probably not more dan a day or two."

"Will you stay with me until help arrives?" Wendell anxiously asked, hoping Reggie would say yes.

"Sure. No problem. But you should get some more sleep. I'll keep watch. If I see any search planes, I'll wake you up."

"Thanks," Wendell said. "I'm really tired."

Once Wendell closed his eyes, Reggie walked down the beach under the light of a full moon and located the raft. Dragging it further away from the jagged lime rock shore, he covered it with brush just before a plane flew overhead and disappeared beyond the horizon. *That was close*, he thought. *With luck, no one will ever know dat Wendell has been here.*

CHAPTER

Acklins Bight, East of Fortune Island, Bahamas

"Let us out," a young Haitian man pleaded as huge storm driven waves slammed against the ship's rusty bulkhead. "We're suffocating. We need fresh air."

"Be patient," the first mate snarled, covering his nose with a handkerchief to filter out the stench of human waste and vomit. "In a few hours we'll be out of sight of American patrol boats and you'll be allowed on deck."

"We can't wait that long," an angry Haitian said in desperation. "Some of the women and children are sick. We haven't seen the sun for over three days. We need to get out of here."

"My baby needs help," a mother screamed as she held up the listless infant for the mate to look at. "He'll suffocate down here. He needs fresh air or he'll die."

"I'll see what I can do," the first mate sneered as he turned his gaze away from the sick child. "No guarantees, but I'll talk ta de captain."

"No more talk!" a tall Haitian man at the back of the crowd yelled.

"Would you like to live in this filth?" called another voice from the rear of the cargo hold. Without warning, a rag full of rotten food splattered against the mate's chest. "We've had enough!"

In a final effort to calm his angry passengers, the mate raised his arms and pleaded with them again. "It'll only be a few more hours, and den we'll be safe. You've already endured so much. Can several more hours be ta high a price ta pay for a chance at getting ta de States?"

"Easy for you to say. It's not your children and parents who are suffering. I don't know about the others, but I can't wait any longer."

"Me either," another yelled. Rushing forward, the angry Haitians cast aside the fearful mate and clamored up the ladder towards the main deck.

Simone and her family were the last to leave. When they arrived at the base of the ladder, Simone discovered a badly bruised old woman in the shadows pleading for help.

"Give me you hand," Simone said. "Let me help you up."

"Thank you." The woman sighed and grabbed hold of Simone's arm.

After lifting the woman up, Simone took a closer look at the woman and asked, "Have we met someplace before?"

"We might have," the woman admitted as she clung to Simone. "I've lived in Haiti all my life. Perhaps you saw me at the market."

"Perhaps," Simone acknowledged.

"Hurry," Claude Joseph urged his daughter as the rest of the family scrambled to the main deck.

Upon exiting the hatch, the Josephs found themselves surrounded by an angry crew. "Get below," one of them yelled as he swung a wooden club at Joseph's head.

"Look out!" Simone screamed.

Deftly stepping sideways, an astonished Claude watched the club strike the ship's rusty bulkhead with a loud thud.

"I'll take care of him," one of the Haitian refugees shouted. Grabbing the man with the club, he socked him in the jaw and knocked him to the deck.

"Head for the rear of the ship," Claude shouted. "It will offer shelter and we can defend ourselves better there."

Nodding their heads, his family followed him down the sea-washed deck.

"I don't think we can make it," Simone's mother yelled.

"We've got to try," Claude yelled. "Anything is better than dying in that filthy cargo hold."

"You're right. But there's so much wind and rain I can barely see," Marie complained.

"I understand, but we need to get to the back of the ship. There's a passageway where we can seek shelter. Use the railing against the bulkhead to guide you. When you get there, you and the children secure yourselves to the railing with this rope I picked up when we left the cargo hold. I'll be right behind you."

"I can't do this," the trembling old woman sobbed as she clung to Simone.

"You've got to. Promise me you won't let go of my arm."

"I don't know if I'm strong enough to hold on. I'm too weak," the woman moaned. "It would be better if you let go of me and saved yourself."

"I won't do that." Simone tightened her grip around the woman's slender waist and prayed that they'd all make it to the stern. The blinding rain whipping against their faces made it difficult to see, and several times Simone felt that she would lose her grip and the old woman would be washed overboard.

"It was very courageous of you to help me," the old woman sobbed as they reached the safety of the passageway. Lifting a small cloth bag from around her neck she placed it in Simone's hand. "If for some reason I don't survive this trip, I want you to have this. It's been in my family for a very long time. It's the least I can offer you for trying to save my life."

"What is it?" Simone studied the small, plaid flannel sack the old woman had handed her.

"It contains an amulet with special powers. A powerful voodoo priest gave it to my family when I was a young girl. It always protected us whenever we got into trouble. Now I want it to do the same for you."

Smiling, Simone promised to wear the sack around her neck and hoped the amulet's powers were as strong as the old woman claimed. She didn't believe in voodoo, but right now, she was willing to accept all the help she and her family could get.

CHAPTER

Landrail, Crooked Island

"I can't find Reggie anywhere," a distraught Lewis Garland said to his wife, Margaret, after mooring his boat to their dock. "I should have known he'd try something like dis. Dat boy is as strong-willed as his old man."

"You can't blame yourself. You don't suppose anything could have happened ta him during de storm?"

"I hope not," Lewis said. Climbing up the ladder to the top of the dock, he turned and looked out over the water. "It was pretty nasty out der. I know de *Sea Star* is a sturdy boat, but I don't know if she's built ta make it through dat kind of weather."

"Let's pray dat she is," Margaret said. Walking towards the end of the dock, they held each other's hands. "Did you check all de places he likes ta hang out?"

"Yeah, I visited most of his friends. Nobody's seen or heard from him."

"What do we do now?" Margaret wiped a tear from her cheek.

"I'm going ta let de police know dat he's run away. I'll drive ta der office while you're making dinner fer de children. Maybe dey'll have more success tracking him down. I'm also going ta ask some of de local fishermen ta help out. If we're lucky, one of dem might spot him when dey are out on de water tomorrow."

"I've heard dat dey are sending out a search team ta look fer a pilot and boy whose plane crashed nearby in a storm," Margaret said. "Maybe dey can spot Reggie while dey are looking fer de others."

"Dat's true." Lewis nodded his head, "When I talk to de police, I'll suggest dat dey contact de pilots of de search plane and have dem look fer Reggie while dey're flying over de crash site."

CHAPTER

Japapa's Camp, North End of Fortune Island

The moment was almost at hand. It had been almost thirteen grueling years since Japapa had escaped from Port-au-Prince and set up his drug smuggling operation in the Bahamas. Now he was on the verge of making his triumphant return to Haiti. He had all the money and power he needed to get himself elected as his country's next president. There were only a few minor details he needed to take care of before carrying out the last phase of his plan. Stepping outside his hut, he glared at the two spies who had just returned from Port-au-Prince. "Are you certain Claude Joseph has left the country?"

"Yes. He and his family boarded the ship several days ago," one of the spies acknowledged.

"And the captain? Can he be trusted to do what we asked?"

"Absolutely, we've paid him extremely well. I can assure you he'll carry out your instructions to deliver Joseph and his daughter into your hands. What are your plans for his wife and son and the others on board the ship?"

"His wife is no threat to me. The men can have her and the other women on board. The rest you can dispose of any way you see fit," Japapa snarled. "I have special plans for Mr. Joseph and his attractive young daughter." Grinning with satisfaction, the priest turned and spoke to his assistant, Peter, who was standing by his side. "I understand you took care of Mr. Sands and his family?"

"Yes. Both Mr. and Mrs. Sands are dead. I set it up as a hit-and-run accident. I doubt anyone suspects it was murder. I've since paid off the police and gotten the driver released from jail. I regret to say their son, Reggie, is still alive, but I'm certain he won't create problems."

"Let's hope not. I couldn't afford having that family homesteading on the south side of Fortune Island. Sooner or later, they would have given us trouble. Eventually, I'll have to deal with the old fisherman who's living there. I also understand that a charter plane carrying medical supplies has crashed somewhere nearby. I want you to send some men to locate it before the authorities find it. I need to get hold of those supplies. Some of our men are pretty banged up after our last run-in with the American patrol boat."

"What if they find survivors when they get to the plane?" Peter asked.

"Make sure there are none when they leave," Japapa snarled.

CHAPTER

Goat Cay, the Following Day

"Time ta get up," Reggie barked as he leaned over and shook Wendell's shoulder. "I've speared some fish fer breakfast."

Removing the sleepers from the corners of his eyes, Wendell turned around and shielded them from the morning sun. "What time is it?" he moaned.

"I don't know, Mon. I don't own a watch. But de sun's been up fer a while. My guess is dat its about nine o'clock." Reggie kneeled and started filleting fish on a flat piece of driftwood that floated ashore after the storm.

"I still hurt all over," Wendell groaned as he tried to sit up. "What kind of fish are they?" he asked as Reggie skinned and removed the bones from one of them. "They're different from the ones I see in the fish markets in New York."

"De blue and gold one is a queen triggerfish, and de brown one with de weird looking teeth is a hogfish. I was hoping ta spear a grouper, but de only one I saw swam under some coral before I could get it."

"Well, I'm starving." Wendell sighed and gingerly stood up. "Is there anything I can do to help?"

"Yea, Mon, get some wood fer de fire. Make sure dat it's dry; otherwise, it won't burn. I suggest you search under de bushes on de backside of de dune. I found plenty der earlier. While you're doing dat, I'll finish filleting de fish and collect some ripe sea grapes."

"All right." Trudging slowly inland, Wendell began searching under the protective canopies of Australian pines and thatch palms. It didn't take him too long to find what he needed. There was an abundance of dry twigs and limbs scattered about by the storm. "Is this enough?" Wendell asked when he returned with his third load.

"Plenty," Reggie smiled and offered Wendell some purple grapes. "Try dese. Dey'll take away de dry taste you have in your mouth in de morning."

"Thanks," Wendell said as he eagerly bit into the marble-size fruit and grimaced. "What's in the middle of this thing anyway?"

"Dat's de seed." Reggie grinned as he placed a couple more fruit into his mouth. "Just eat de soft part and spit out de rest."

"There's not a lot of flesh on them," Wendell whined. "A person could starve to death if he had to survive on these things. How long will it take to cook the fish?"

"Not long." Reggie raised his eyes and shook his head before offering Wendell the last of the sea grapes and stoking the fire.

"No thanks. I think I'll wait for the fish." Wendell waved away Reggie's offer of grapes and anxiously waited for the fish to finish cooking. "I guess you didn't see any search planes while I was asleep?"

"No, Mon, I didn't see nothin'."

"That's too bad," Wendell sighed. "I thought someone would have flown over by now. What about the raft? Were you able to pull it further away from the water's edge?"

"Yeah, but I'm afraid I didn't drag it up far enough, and when de tide came in it drifted off. I was hoping dat it might have washed up on one of de nearby beaches, but I didn't see it anywhere."

"Great!" Wendell groaned. "Without the raft, how will the search planes spot me from the air? Let's put another pile of wood together and create a bigger fire to attract them."

"I've been thinking about dat." Reggie scratched his head and gave Wendell a sheepish look. "How would you like ta sail with me ta Fortune Island? You could help me get settled. Den after I've moved in ta my new home, I'll take you back ta de mainland with my boat. You'll be doing me a big favor and it won't take dat long."

"But I don't want to go to Fortune Island. Why can't you take me to Crooked Island today?" Wendell pleaded. "My mother and father must be worried sick about me. They might even give you a reward for bringing me back."

"Mon, I wish I could do dat," Reggie sighed, "but I can't."

"What do you mean you can't?"

"I've run away. If I show up on Crooked, my uncle will find me and he won't like de idea of me living by myself on Fortune Island. He'll want ta send me back ta Nassau ta live with my aunt. It's just too risky ta bring you back now."

"Swell. And when the drones, planes and patrol boats can't find me, everyone will think I'm dead."

"Dey might," Reggie admitted, "but I can't risk anyone finding me. Besides, if I take you back now, what kind of guarantee would I have dat you won't tell de police where I am? Der bound ta ask you lots of questions."

"I promise. I won't tell them a thing. You could help me make up a story they'd believe. I could tell them I got knocked on the head when the plane crashed and couldn't remember anything after that."

"And how would you explain winding up on Crooked Island when de plane crashed offshore?" Reggie asked.

"I could say that a fisherman rescued me."

"Who'd believe dat story? De first thing de police would want ta know is de name of de fisherman so dey could ask him questions."

"Great. Kidnapped by a runaway who likes to eat lizards and snails. What a swell way to spend the Christmas holidays," Wendell grouched.

"Sorry," Reggie said as he handed Wendell a fish filet on a sea grape leaf. "Look at it dis way. If you were me, would you be willing ta let me go?"

"Probably not. But don't count on me hanging around. The first chance I get I'm out of here."

"Without a boat you won't get very far. Maybe after a day or so you'll see things differently."

"I doubt it," Wendell grumbled as he devoured Reggie's fish and tossed the sea grape leaf into the bushes. "What do you mean 'get settled' and 'move in'?" How can you start a life on land you don't own? And you're only fooling yourself if you think your uncle is going to give up looking for you."

"I thought about dat too. I plan ta make it look like my boat sank and I drowned."

"That's crazy. You'd be a lot better off moving to Nassau to live with your aunt and return to Crooked when you're older. Then, you could become a fishing guide, and if you do well, you could probably buy the land you want to live on."

"Do you know how long dat would take?" Reggie shot back. "I don't want ta wait fifteen years. By den some developer will buy de property my family dreamed of living on. If I take you back now, any chance of making my family's dream come true would be gone forever."

"I hear you," Wendell responded, "but you sure aren't going to make your folks' plans a reality by kidnapping me and settling on property you don't own. Maybe you could buy the land with your folks' life insurance money," Wendell suggested.

"Fat chance; dey didn't have any, and de person dat caused de accident took off after he was released on bail, so I won't be getting any money from him."

"Well, kidnapping me isn't the solution," Wendell retorted. "Someone is bound to find you and put you in jail for what you're doing. Then what happens to your future?"

"Dat ain't going ta happen, not if I play my cards right," Reggie boasted as he put some more fish on the fire and looked out across the water in the direction of Fortune Island.

CHAPTER

Early Morning, West of Fortune Island

"Is dat de last of dem?" the Bahamian captain snarled and shook his head in disgust.

Eight more Haitians were being shoved aboard a small life raft, much to the delight of the crew.

"Yes, sir," the mate replied. "I'm sure glad ta see dat lot of troublemakers go."

"We all are," the captain testily replied. "What about Claude Joseph and his family? Did dey survive?"

"Yes."

"Good. I wouldn't want anything ta happen ta dem. Radio Japapa and give him de coordinates where dey and de rest of dis motley bunch can be picked up."

"Aye, aye."

"What does he want?" the captain grunted. Looking down at one of the life rafts, he pointed to a Haitian frantically waving his arms.

"He wants some paddles so dey can row ta one of de nearby islands."

"Tell him I don't have any. He'll have ta paddle with his hands if he expects ta make it ta one of de islands," the captain chuckled before heading towards the bridge. "I'm sure dat Japapa and his men will pick dem up shortly. Den they'll find out what a living hell is really like."

After hearing the captain's response, one of the seamen shoved the last raft away from the stern, and the captain ordered the crew to start up the engines. The fighting aboard the ship had lasted for over an hour. Nine Haitians and two Bahamians had lost their lives and the captain was in no mood to show any mercy. At first, Simone thought that he was going to toss all of them over the side, but for some unexplained reason he ordered them set adrift.

"Where's the old woman?" Simone asked her father as their raft drifted away from the cargo ship. "When I got separated from you, I lost track of her."

"I don't know." Claude looked around the overcrowded life raft. "Probably in one of the other boats."

"Have you seen an old woman?" Simone asked the distraught young mother seated alongside her. Without saying a word, the woman shook her head and wrapped her arms around her infant.

"She was wearing a tattered brown dress and a colorful bandana around her head," Simone continued before pausing.

Looking at the child, she realized that all the color was gone from its face. Tears welled up in her eyes as she turned towards her father and whispered, "I think her baby is dead."

Claude looked over at the woman and her infant and nodded.

"Is there anything we can do to help?" Simone whispered.

"I'm afraid not," Simone's father said.

Cradling the infant's lifeless body, the mother began singing a familiar Haitian lullaby. "Soon, we'll all need help," Claude sighed as everyone on board listened to the woman's mournful tune with tears in their eyes. "There's no food or water on this raft, and without paddles, we may never reach shore."

Cresting waves, produced by a nearby storm, poured gallons of seawater into the tiny rafts. For hours, the frantic refugees used their hands to scoop water out of the sinking vessels, but by midafternoon everyone had given up. Too tired to continue, it was apparent their fate had been sealed. Then one of the young men stood up and pointed. "Land," he shouted. "I see land."

"Where?" an old man asked.

"Over there," he yelled pointing north. "The current is moving in the right direction and we can use our hands to paddle towards the island."

At first, only a few of the weary Haitians responded to the man's desperate pleas. But enthusiasm mounted as the island drew closer. "We're going to make it," a relieved woman shouted. "I can see the beach."

"I can too," another cried.

"Thank God!" someone else yelled as renewed hope spread throughout the group.

"Don't do it!" Simone's mother screamed.

Everyone turned and stared. "Someone grab her," Simone's father pleaded as he lurched forward and tried to grab hold of the young woman and her child. But it was too late. The woman and her infant slipped off the edge of the raft. Determined to prevent them from drowning, Simone jumped into the water and tried to rescue them, but her efforts were in vain. Quickly engulfed by the cresting waves, the mother and her infant disappeared beneath the blanket of deep blue water.

"What was her name?" a distraught woman sitting next to Simone's father asked as she stared over the side in disbelief.

"I don't know," he lamented with tears running down his cheeks. "I only wish there was something we could have done to help."

"There was nothing any of us could have done. She just couldn't bear the thought of living without her child," the woman sighed.

Claude nodded in agreement as he reached over the side and pulled Simone on board the raft.

CHAPTER

16

Rescue Plane South of French Wells

"Base to Rescue One. Have you seen any sign of wreckage?"

"Negative, Base," the pilot responded as he continued to scan the surface of the water for signs of debris. "We've covered most of the area where the pilot reported going down, but we still haven't seen anything. We're going to stay here a little longer and then head south. It's possible his GPS wasn't working properly and he gave us the wrong coordinates."

"Roger, Rescue One."

"Look! Over there," the copilot, Raul Gomez, interrupted. "It looks like there are life rafts loaded with people."

Lowering their altitude to get a better look, the two rescue workers spotted a cluster of inflated vessels being swept over a fringing reef and hurled towards the sandy shore of a small island.

"Rescue One to Base. We've just spotted several rafts filled with what appear to be Haitian refugees being washed ashore near Lucian Cay south of French Wells."

"Roger, Rescue One. How many people do you estimate there are?"

"At least forty. A lot appear to be women and children."

"Acknowledged, Rescue One. We'll inform the Bahamian authorities. They'll want to round them up."

"Poor souls," Gomez said after he completed his transmission. "I really feel sorry for them. My family and I escaped from Cuba in a small boat. We were lucky. We made it ashore in the Florida Keys. These people have risked everything to get to the United States, but I'm afraid there's little hope of that happening now."

"I agree," the pilot said and turned the plane towards the south. "As illegal immigrants, the Bahamian government will ship them back to Haiti. Since they probably spent all the money they had to make this journey, they'll be worse off when they get deported. Many of their homes were destroyed after the earthquake and their government is still having a hard time recuperating. The captain that did this to them should be sent to prison."

"Maybe he will be," Raul sighed, "but I doubt it."

"As we head south, let's also keep our eyes out for that runaway. The police chief said his uncle was pretty upset. The boy had just lost his parents in a car accident and he's concerned that the young man may do something foolish."

CHAPTER

Goat Cay

Wendell watched and waited. Lying on his back, he surveyed the star-filled sky that stretched across the horizon. He never realized the Milky Way was so beautiful. Even on the clearest evenings, it wasn't something he could see in the hazy, light-saturated sky above New York City.

Across from him, Reggie mumbled in his sleep. He was trying to warn his parents about an approaching vehicle. Thrashing about, he suddenly bolted upright and yelled, "Look out!"

"Are you all right?" Wendell asked.

Sweat poured from Reggie's brow. Totally oblivious of Wendell's presence, he stared into the distance, then lay back down and resumed his troubled sleep.

The rhythmic pounding of the surf and the sweet smell of night-blooming jasmine nearly lulled Wendell to sleep. He was beginning to believe that the right moment for him to escape would never arrive. Finally, Reggie stopped mumbling, his breathing became shallower, and he appeared to enter a deep sleep. It was now or never. Quietly lifting himself up, Wendell headed down the beach towards Reggie's boat. He didn't know much about sailing, but he knew the *Sea Star* was his only hope of getting home.

Once he got away from the island, he hoped one of the search planes or a drone would spot him. Even better, he might encounter a local fisherman. At the water's edge, he stopped to hear if Reggie was following. Except for the scented breeze blowing through the palm trees and the rhythmic ocean waves lapping against the sandy beach, there were no other sounds. Wading out to the *Sea Star*, Wendell hoisted himself on board and pulled up the anchor. The tide was going out and all he had to do was use the boat's wooden paddle to shove it into deeper water. Everything appeared to be going fine until he heard a loud splash.

"Planning ta go someplace?" Reggie grinned. Grabbing hold of the *Sea Star's* stern, he stopped the boat's forward motion and glared at Wendell.

"Let go," Wendell shouted as he tried to dislodge Reggie's grip with the boat's oar.

"Nice try," Reggie yelled as he took hold of the wooden paddle and yanked Wendell overboard. "Did you really think you could get away dat easily?"

"It was worth a try," Wendell sputtered. Standing up, he tried to wrestle the boat back from Reggie.

"Well, you've missed your chance," Reggie said as he shoved Wendell back down into the water. "In de morning, we're sailing ta Fortune Island."

"Swell," Wendell grumbled as he followed Reggie back to the beach. "And what about the search planes and drones? I'll bet one of them will spot your boat and have someone check you out."

I've thought about dat," Reggie admitted, "but it seems dey've stopped looking in dis area fer de time being ."

"You seem to have thought of everything," Wendell testily responded as he stomped ashore.

"I would think you would be pleased with de idea of traveling ta Fortune Island," Reggie said with a smirk. "I told you before dat once I get things set up on de island, I'll figure out a way ta take you back ta Crooked."

"So, you say. And how long is that going to take? By the time you figure out how to do it, I'll be an old man."

"I hope not, Mon. The thought of spending de rest of my life with you really doesn't appeal ta me either. Sometimes, I think I should have left you on dos rocks."

"Maybe you should have. And next time, I'll make sure I don't crash land anywhere near you."

"Too bad you didn't think about dat sooner," Reggie grumbled.

"You're a selfish jerk." Wendell kicked the sand in frustration and followed Reggie back across the dune to their camp. "Do you ever think of anyone but yourself?"

Clenching his fists, Reggie turned and glared at Wendell. "So, you think I'm a selfish jerk," Reggie yelled. "If it wasn't fer me, you'd still be stranded on dat rocky beach with no food or water. And who fixed your wounds when you were in pain? Your parents are still alive, but my mother and father are dead. Have you ever been in an accident and lost everyone you loved? Now I have nothin' else ta look forward ta except making der dream a reality. I don't think you have any right ta judge whether or not I'm a selfish jerk."

"Maybe not," Wendell admitted, "but fulfilling your parents' dream is no excuse for holding me hostage. Besides, I don't like the idea of being stuck out here with you anymore than you do. I could think of a lot better places to be over the Christmas holidays, like being with friends from school playing basketball in the gym or ice skating in Central Park. Now I've got nothin' to look forward to but spending the rest of my life with you."

CHAPTER

Haitian Refugees on Lucian Cay, Bahamas

"I can't believe we made it," Simone said to her father as she and her brother helped pull the last of the rafts up onto the beach.

"I agree; it's a miracle. Now that we're here, I want you and your brother to scout around and see if you can find some food," Claude Joseph told his children. "Here's some flashlights I found in the rafts. Your mom and I and the others will use the kits from the rafts to repair any that were damaged. We'll also collect some driftwood that we can make into paddles. I'm sure the plane we spotted earlier has already reported us to the authorities, so we'll need to get off this island as quick as possible."

"How long do you think it will be before someone shows up?" Simone asked.

"That's hard to say. They might send a patrol boat tomorrow. If we're lucky, we'll be out of here before daybreak.

One thing is certain—we can't afford to get caught and sent back to Haiti."

"We won't let that happen," Simone's younger brother declared.

"That's what I like to hear." Claude smiled. "There's only a few hours before darkness sets in, so you better get started."

Gathering food was easier than Simone and her younger brother anticipated. There were dozens of mature pink conchs in the grass flats near shore, and they were able to harvest lots of large West Indian top shells from under the lime rock ledge near the beach. They also collected coconuts that had dropped from the nearby palm trees. The milk inside the nuts would provide enough liquid to help prevent dehydration until they found a better source of water, and the nuts' sweet meat would supplement their diet of snails.

Scanning the beach with his flashlight, Michael made the best find of all—sea turtle tracks leading into the dune. Jumping up and down, he shouted to his sister to hurry.

"What is it?" Simone asked, panting as she caught up with her brother. Taking a moment to catch her breath, she slowly searched the beach with her flashlight to see what her brother had discovered.

"Turtle tracks," he shouted. "Look! They lead to the top of the sand dune. I'll bet she laid her eggs behind that clump of bushes."

"You're probably right. Let's see if we can find them."

Eagerly following the tracks, they soon discovered a matted area behind the dune. "This looks like the spot," Michael shouted. Kneeling, he began clawing into the cool sand.

"Let me help," Simone said and excitedly began digging at the sand covering the nest.

"I think I feel one," Michael yelled.

"Where? I don't see anything," Simone said as she picked up her flashlight and pointed it into the cavity they'd created.

"Right there," Michael yelled as he cleared away more sand. "Can't you see them? There seems to be a whole bunch clustered together."

"You're right. Dad will really be proud of you."

There were seventy eggs in the nest, and it took Simone and her brother a half dozen trips to the rafts to bring back all the food they'd gathered.

"You two did great," Claude announced with pride when Simone and Michael arrived with the last load. "It looks like our situation might not be as hopeless as I first feared. While you and the other children were out finding food, some of the men and I were able to locate enough wood to make the paddles we need."

"How soon before we leave?" Michael asked.

"Not long," Claude responded. "Probably sometime in the early morning. It's best to leave under the cover of darkness. That way, the search planes and patrol boats will have a harder time spotting us."

"Have you come up with a plan to get us to the States?" Simone asked her father as she and her brother followed him up the beach to help prepare the first decent meal the refugees had had in days.

"Not yet." Claude shook his head. "Some want to head to Great Exuma to see if we can find a captain who'd be willing to drop us off in the Florida Keys. I'm not so sure that will work. Any captain we contact will want to be paid for the risk he'd be taking, and none of us have any money to pay him. In addition, the United States Government is not keen on taking in more refugees at the moment, so there will be a lot of patrol boats looking for us. Canada will be our safest haven, but it's a long distance from here and we've got to figure out how to get there."

CHAPTER

Colonel Hill Police Station, Crooked Island

"Have you any idea where Reggie might have taken off ta?" the tall, good-looking, Crooked Island police chief asked Lewis Garland from behind a well-worn wooden desk. The officer was dressed in a freshly pressed white shirt and black pants and his concerned demeanor gave Lewis the feeling he could count on the man's help.

"I thought I did." Lewis responded as the police station's squeaky ceiling fan labored uselessly over their heads. "I checked de old fishing camp he and his father used ta visit. I also talked ta nearly all of his friends. He wasn't at de camp, and none of his friends had any idea where he might have run off ta. I really appreciate dat you agreed ta help me find him when I called you earlier. I know everyone's busy looking fer survivors of dat plane crash and asking you ta find my nephew only places an extra burden on you."

"Dat's not a problem. Perhaps we can pool our resources and work together. I'm going ta spend the next few days searching de waters around Fish Cay fer signs of de downed plane. While I'm der, I'll keep a lookout fer Reggie. If you and some of de other fishermen would explore de waters around French Wells, Old Woman Cay, and Black Rock, it would cut down on de area I would have ta cover and we might get lucky. So far, all de search plane has spotted are some refugees near Lucian Cay. I don't have time ta deal with dem now, so I've notified de authorities in Nassau ta pick dem up."

"Sounds like a good plan ta me. I'll talk ta de search party of fishermen I've pulled together. I feel bad about what's happened. I should have paid more attention ta Reggie, but after my sister and her husband died in dat terrible car accident, I got all tied up in paperwork and de funeral arrangements."

"I understand, but you can't blame yourself fer what's happened. You did de best you could under de circumstances."

"I suppose," Lewis sighed, "but I'll never forgive myself if something happens ta Reggie."

"I'm sure we'll find him." The police chief pushed his chair back and stood up. "Why don't you walk with me ta de airport across de way. I'm headed over ta talk ta some local officials. Der anxious ta know if de search plane spotted any sign of de wreckage. When I finish with dem, I need ta speak ta a sport fisherman who called me last night."

"Thanks, fer de offer, but I better head back home. My wife and de rest of de family will be anxious ta hear about your plan, and I need ta get in touch with de other fishermen as soon as possible."

As the two men stepped out the front door of the small, newly painted police station they were greeted by a narrow band of orange light streaming between blankets of purple clouds. "Looks like tomorrow is going ta be a nice day," the chief observed. "Let's hope it will be a more successful one." Nodding his agreement, Lewis shook hands with the chief and walked to his car on the recently paved road under the late afternoon shadows of Australian pines.

CHAPTER

New York Airport, The Day After the Crash

"Ben and I are in the New York airport. When we get to Fort Lauderdale, we'll take a charter plane to Crooked," Wendell's mom shouted to her father, Wilson Cooper, over the cell phone. "I'm sorry, I can barely hear you." She pressed the phone closer to her ear so she could block out the sounds of laughter coming from a group of children who were playing near the front desk.

"No, Amy isn't with us. We left her with Ben's parents. If there are no delays, we should arrive on Crooked Island about one this afternoon. Yes, the company is continuing the search. However, they're not very optimistic about finding anybody alive. We hope they're wrong. They told us they'd like to locate the plane and find out the reason it crashed. Will you meet us at the airport when we arrive? . . . . Good. Is there anything you want us to bring? . . . . Ok. I love you too. Bye."

"How is he?" Ben asked after Emily turned off her cell phone.

"He appears to be holding up okay under the circumstances. He doesn't say much but I can tell he's really upset. He said he doesn't need anything—only wants us to get there as soon as possible."

"Still no sign of the plane?"

"No. He said nearly everyone on the island is looking for it. It seems a boy named Reggie ran away from home about the same time the plane went down. They plan to search for both boys as well as the pilot. I feel so helpless," Emily sobbed and rested her head against her husband's chest.

Ben stroked his wife's hair and tried to hold back his own tears. "We can't lose hope. Do you know anything about this other boy they're looking for?"

"Dad said he's the son of a couple I went to school with when I was growing up on the island. Both parents died a little more than a week ago in an auto accident in Nassau."

"In one way it's kind of fortunate he ran away," Ben reflected.

"What do you mean?" Emily lifted her head and stared at her husband.

"Only that, if this boy, Reggie, hadn't run away we might not have as many people out searching for Wendell and the plane."

"You're probably right. I never thought about that."

Ben nodded toward a group of excited vacationers lining up at the gate. "I think it's time to board the plane."

Numbed by recent events, the weary couple made their way towards the departure gate. Outside the terminal window, workers were still attempting to clear snow deposited by a recent cold front. Hopefully, the weather wouldn't delay their flight.

CHAPTER

South End of Fortune Island

"Dat's de south end of Fortune Island," Reggie shouted and gleefully pointed towards the approaching shoreline. Meanwhile, Wendell desperately clung to his seat while wind-driven waves slammed into the sailboat. "We're headed ta a cove behind dos rocks. De entrance is really narrow and it will be a little tricky ta maneuver through it."

Wendell bit his lower lip and grimaced. Salt spray bit into the cuts on his face and arms, and no matter which way he turned, he failed to get relief. Once again, he felt disgusted with himself for being so inept at trying to escape earlier. "Are you sure you know how to get through?"

"No problem. Trust me, Mon."

Before Wendell could protest, a large wave lifted the *Sea Star* up and catapulted it towards a steep bluff. The roar from cresting waves pounding against the cliff enveloped them in a thunderous blanket of imminent doom. Frozen with fear, Wendell gripped the side of the boat and closed his eyes waiting for the boat to be dashed against the rocks.

"You can open your eyes now," Reggie laughed as the last wave swooped them past some protruding rocks into the lagoon. Wendell was shocked to find himself still in one piece. "I told you it wouldn't be a problem. I'm used ta guiding de *Sea Star* through tight places."

Shaking his head, Wendell wiped the salt spray from his face and surveyed their surroundings. Before him lay a palm-lined shore whose brilliant sandy beach was fringed by one crystal clear, emerald green body of water. He'd seen pictures of places like this in his parents' travel brochures but he never thought they really existed.

"Wow! This place is awesome," Wendell grudgingly admitted.

"Yeah. It's just like I remember it. Dis lagoon is loaded with fish and lobster so der'll be plenty of food fer us ta eat. Before I head fer shore, I'm going ta scout out de area ta see if der's someplace I can hide de boat."

The wind eased inside the lagoon and the *Sea Star* glided over the glistening waters. Shading his eyes from the sun, Reggie scanned the beach looking for a place to hide his boat. He rejected several potential sites and finally spotted a mangrove creek at the north end of the cove and headed towards it.

"When I get inside de creek," Reggie yelled to Wendell, "I want you ta drop de anchor over. The trees dat hang over de creek will prevent anyone from spotting my boat from de air."

"How nice," Wendell replied sarcastically. Reluctantly, he picked up the anchor and waited for Reggie to maneuver the vessel into the narrow channel. As soon as they entered the creek, fish with dark colored bands running across their eyes began darting everywhere. "What are those?" a curious Wendell asked.

"Snappers," Reggie said. Slowing the boat's forward motion, he ordered Wendell to throw the anchor over the side. "Later, when we get settled, I'll catch some fer dinner. Right now, we need ta unload everything and locate de abandoned house my father discovered. I'd like ta move into it as soon as possible."

"It won't be soon enough for me," Wendell said. After dropping the anchor into the creek and securing it to the bottom, he began swatting at the hordes of mosquitoes that quickly enveloped them. "God this place is awful. I've never seen so many mosquitoes in my life. How can you stand it? Is the house close by?" Wendell sputtered as he clamored over the side of the boat trying to get away from the aggravating cloud of bugs being sucked into his mouth and nose.

"About a half mile or less. You can help by taking some of dos cooking supplies ta de top of de sand dune on de other side of de trees. I'll bring de tent and some of de other gear."

Before grabbing the pots and pans, Wendell brushed away several dozen mosquitoes that were blanketing his arms and blew half a dozen more out of his nose. "I hope there are fewer bugs up there," he complained before hastily hauling the cooking supplies away from the creek.

"Der will be," Reggie chuckled. Gathering the rest of the supplies, he quickly followed Wendell out of the mangroves.

Near the top of the dune, Wendell took another moment to stare at the spectacular view. Row after row of bent coconut palms lined the perimeter of the lagoon, their long slender trunks arching majestically over the glistening sand. Inside the lagoon, a gentle breeze caressed the palm fronds, and the air was saturated with the dizzying aromas of honeysuckle and sweet acacia.

"It's de Garden of Eden," Reggie announced when he reached the place where Wendell was standing. "Dad said der wasn't another place like it on Earth."

"I'd believe you if it wasn't for the bugs," Wendell grouched.

"Dis place used ta be a coconut plantation," Reggie explained as he put down the rest of his gear. "Some people in de States bought de land back in 1946 and tried ta make a go of it, but dey ran out of money. Later, dey sold it ta a development company who wanted ta turn it inta a tourist resort. Dat company went bankrupt, and since den no one's been back."

"I'm glad." Wendell sighed and focused on a red and green hummingbird hovering above a cluster of red coral bean flowers. "It's hard to believe anyone could improve upon the beauty of this island."

"Dat's for sure. But we'll have plenty of time ta enjoy de view later. Der's a trail leading away from de beach over der by dos trees. If we're lucky it will lead ta de place my father planned ta buy. De house is situated at de top of da hill."

"Why would anyone want to build up there?" Wendell asked. Taking one last look at the lagoon, he shook his head in amazement before following Reggie along the trail. "I'd build my home next to the beach. I don't think I'd ever get tired of that view."

"Me either, Mon. But when de wind stops blowin' or it comes from de opposite direction, de skeeters and sand flies would eat you alive down der."

"I hadn't thought about that," Wendell panted as he tried to keep up with Reggie who was anxious to get to the top of the hill. "But I have to agree that more bugs could make things pretty miserable."

"Der's de house!" Reggie said, excitedly pointing to an overgrown structure in the clearing ahead of them.

"It doesn't look like it's in very good shape." Wendell gasped and bent over as he reached the top of the hill.

"We'll be able ta fix it up. De walls and windows are in good shape. All it needs is a new roof."

"Is that all!?" Wendell groaned. "And where do you think you're going to get the lumber to build a new one?"

"No problem. Der's always lots of it washed up on de windward side of de island after winter storms. Some of it gets washed off freighters."

"How exciting. I can't wait to spend the next couple of months hauling lumber up this hill so you can put on a new roof."

"It won't take dat long, . . . Reggie paused and pointed to some bushes. "Did you hear dat?"

Straining to listen, Wendell peered at the bushes and shook his head. "I don't hear anything. Are you sure it's not the wind?"

"I'm sure, Mon. I think it's some kind of animal."

"I don't see anything," Wendell said and nervously kept looking around.

"Der he is!" Reggie shouted as a huge, black, bristly-haired pig with five-inch tusks emerged from behind a tree.

"Do you think someone owns him?" Wendell asked.

"No, Mon. He's a wild boar and dey can be real mean."

"Great," Wendell groaned as he stared at the snorting beast. "How did he get on the island?"

"I haven't a clue, but you better climb up de nearest tree or you'll be dead meat."

Before Wendell could act, the boar slammed into him and hurled him into the bushes.

"Get up!" Reggie shouted. "He's going ta charge again. Climb into de tree next ta you!"

Dazed and in pain, Wendell staggered towards the tree just as the pig attempted to spear him with its razor-sharp tusks. Luckily, the animal missed, and an incredulous Wendell watched as the huge boar veered off to one side and pawed the ground in frustration. If he didn't hoist himself into the tree soon, he wouldn't have to worry about getting to Crooked Island. Clawing his way up the nearest tree trunk, he grabbed the closest limb and tried to pull himself further away from the ground.

"Higher!" Reggie shouted.

But Wendell's hands slipped on the limb's smooth bark and the boar's tusks snagged his trousers. Wendell gritted his teeth and pulled with all his might as the pig yanked back. It was no use. The boar was winning. Wendell could feel his fingers losing their grip. One last tug and it would all be over. Using his arm to lift himself up, Wendell pulled back with every ounce of strength he could muster. Luck was with him. His pants ripped free of the boar's tusks and the animal tumbled backwards. As Wendell scrambled further up the tree, the frustrated boar squealed and pawed the ground.

"That was close. What now?" Wendell shouted to Reggie who was perched in a nearby tree.

"We stay here and wait him out," Reggie replied. "Hopefully, he'll get bored and go away."

"Swell. I always wanted to spend a night in a tree and live like a squirrel. Are there any nuts up here for me to eat?" Wendell asked sarcastically.

CHAPTER

Haitian Refugees on Lucian Cay

Dressed in a silk wedding gown, Simone found herself standing in front of the old woman from the boat. She was urging Simone to run. "Run where?" she frantically asked. Suddenly a firm hand reached out and grabbed her by the shoulder.

"Wake up!" Claude Joseph shouted. "The police have found us. We must leave."

Struggling to her feet, Simone could hear the terrified shouts and screams of people running past her in the dark.

"This way," her father urged.

Stumbling across unfamiliar terrain, Simone and her younger brother, Michael, followed their father down the beach while beams of light flashed in front of them.

"Stay where you are!" someone shouted. "We won't hurt you."

"Don't listen to him." Claude waved his arm towards the water. "There's a cave inside the face of that cliff. I found it when the tide was out and I was hunting for driftwood. We can hide there."

"Where's Mama?" Michael sobbed.

"She's headed towards the cave," Claude shouted. Grabbing his son's hand, he pulled him towards the water.

"Halt!" A young man lifted his flashlight and shined it into Claude's eyes.

Realizing they were trapped, Claude dove at the man and wrestled him to the ground. "Run!" he shouted to the children. Muffled gunshots arose from the tangled bodies, followed by a loud cry of pain.

"Daddy! Are you all right?" Simone shouted as she and her brother ran over to see if their father was hurt.

"Grab the girl!" someone yelled. "Don't let her get away."

"I've got her." A strong hand reached out in the darkness and took hold of Simone's arm.

"Let go of me!" Simone yelled as she struggled to free herself. "What's happened to my father?"

In a desperate attempt to free herself, Simone bit the hand of the man holding her. Blood seeped into her mouth and the young man cried out in pain, releasing his grip. Racing towards the spot where her father had fallen, she spotted his blood-soaked body and screamed.

Claude stared into his daughter's eyes and pleaded with her to grab her brother and head for the cave.

"I can't leave you," Simone sobbed.

"You must," Claude moaned as he tried to suck air into his lungs. "You need to catch up with your mother," he gasped. "She'll need you. Hopefully she's made it to the cave by now."

Simone hesitated for a moment then turned and looked for her brother. *He must have taken off for the cave,* she thought as she ran towards the water's edge, with tears running down her cheeks. Plunging into the ocean, she began swimming as far from the shore as possible. Lights scanned the ocean surface pointing in her direction. *Where is the cave?* she wondered. Out of breath, she paused and tried to get her bearings. Across the moonlit water, she spotted the silhouette of a towering lime rock cliff. *The cave has to be there.* As she swam toward it, she continued to hear frantic voices coming from the beach. *Can I make it to safety?* Finally, her hand touched the jagged surface of a rocky outcropping. *Is this the entrance?* Searching with her fingers, she felt a narrow crevice and squirmed through its slender passageway. *Safe at last—but where is the rest of my family?* "Mama!" she cried out several times. But there was no response. Her only reply was the echo of her own voice bouncing off the cave walls.

CHAPTER

South End of Fortune Island

The omens were not good. After staring out across the tranquil waters of the lagoon, the suntanned hermit laid down his flute and offered the yellow and green Amazon parrot perched on his shoulder a fresh piece of fruit. Crooked Island residents knew him as Sharkman but his real name was Jeff Mason. They called him Sharkman because his sloping forehead, large nose, and toothy grin reminded the locals of the reef sharks that prowled the surrounding waters.

When Jeff graduated from high school, he married his high school sweetheart. They had a big wedding and invited all their friends to it. His uncle surprised them by purchasing a home near their parents' place. Working as a mechanic, John made a good salary, and after a year, his wife gave birth to twins, a boy and a girl. Life was good until he was drafted into the Viet Nam War. Things didn't go so well after that. While on patrol, he and his men were ambushed. Everyone but Jeff was killed. The enemy dragged him into the jungle where they tortured him for days. They wanted information he insisted he didn't have, but they didn't' believe him. Finally, they sent him to North Viet Nam where he survived for four years in a living hell. He was released when the war was over, and he returned home only to discover his wife and children had died in a fire. Life had been cruel.

Depressed, he left his hometown and took a variety of jobs in different places. Ultimately, he joined some of his military buddies and they moved to the Bahamas to hunt sharks. Shark fishing paid well and he seldom dwelled on his former life. They hunted mostly bull, tiger, and hammerheads. The men used long lines with pieces of fish attached to steel hooks to catch them. The lines were set out in the evening and retrieved the next morning. Most of the sharks were dead by the time they hoisted them on board, but some survived the ordeal. To avoid being bitten, the fishermen clubbed the sharks to death before transporting them back to camp. To his credit, Sharkman convinced his friends not to hunt sharks in their breeding grounds and whenever they hooked a large female that was still alive he made sure it was released.

Once ashore, the fishermen processed the sharks and sold them to foreign markets. They used steel knives to peel the skin from their bodies and cut out their enlarged livers. The shark skin was used to make sandpaper as well as boots, handbags, and belts. The livers were highly prized by pharmaceutical companies because they are rich in vitamin A. Other companies used the liver oil to make anti-aging cream, lipstick, and sunscreen. Nothing was wasted. The cartilage that made up the skeletons was ground up into a powder and made into an alternative cure for cancer, and the jaws were sold as souvenirs.

As the fishermen worked, they often found fascinating objects in the shark stomachs. Once, it was an entire dog. The animal had no tooth marks on it and apparently had been swallowed whole during a shark feeding frenzy. Another time, a captain's log was retrieved with its cover completely intact. Like the ship's log, many of the objects the animals consumed had no food value. Included among them were cork floats, two-by-fours, sneakers, rubber boots and even empty glass bottles.

Initially, Jeff showed little love for these creatures. He believed that sharks were brutal killing machines whose only value was the profit he made from the sale of their body parts. Over time, however, his opinion changed. The more he studied them, the more he realized the important role they play in the marine environment. Through the consumption of sick and weak fish, they help maintain a healthy population of marine life.

After realizing how valuable sharks were in the natural scheme of things, he decided he should do something to protect them. He began by informing his fishing partners that he no longer wished to hunt sharks. Then, with the help of local islanders, he began a campaign to ban shark fishing throughout the Bahamas. It wasn't an easy task. Although local fisherman, including his friends, eventually agreed to the ban, fishing fleets still came to the islands from other parts of world to hunt them. These fishermen were cruel hunters, who were only interested in the animals' fins. Once, he came upon a small fleet in the sharks' breeding grounds. As he watched, dozens of pregnant females were dragged on board the ships, hot steel blades were used to slice off their fins and their helpless bodies were thrown over the side to drown in a sea of blood. It was a crime against Mother Nature. When the incident was reported to the Bahamian government, shark fishing was officially banned in the islands, and they sent patrol boats to drive the fleets away. Now, they no longer hunted in these waters and the shark and commercial fish populations were returning to what they once were.

Sharkman loved the Bahamas and its surrounding waters. Life was good among these subtropical islands and he no longer had any desire to return to the States. He looked forward to spending his days fishing the tranquil waters and exploring the coral reefs. The frothy turbulence of passing storms, the majestic sunsets and the brilliant blue waters encompassing the region's glistening sand beaches filled his soul with contentment. It was a level of peace he knew he'd never find anywhere else on the planet.

Today, however, the fisherman's mind was focused on unsettling developments that had recently taken place on Fortune Island. Ruthless, evil men had set up camp on its northern end. They were drug smugglers, bent on making a fortune. From what he learned; they would stop at nothing to achieve their objective. And then there were the *Chogers*, spirits allegedly responsible for killing some of the local islanders. Initially, he didn't believe they existed, but there were too many unexplained deaths in recent years not to take the stories circulating about them seriously. If he wanted to remain in these islands for the rest of his life, he would have to deal with these threats, and he suspected they would prove to be far more difficult to handle than any of the dangers he encountered while shark fishing.

"Beware of *Chogers*," Sharkman's parrot squawked. Prancing back and forth across the old man's shoulders, it bobbed its head up and down and snatched a piece of fruit from the fisherman's hand.

"Not tonight," the fisherman acknowledged, "but soon. I can see the bubbles rising to the surface and the mist gathering offshore. It won't be long before the *Chogers* make their presence known. I feel them in my bones." Lifting the agitated bird off his shoulder, Sharkman placed him on a dead tree limb before heading into his hut.

"We must all beware," he mumbled to himself, "but there are things I need to do before they come. Tomorrow, I'll begin by trying to warn the young boys that arrived yesterday."

Fortune Island the Following Day

Wendell and Reggie had spent a sleepless night in the trees, too frightened to climb down. It wasn't until the sun came up that they realized the boar had disappeared. "Time ta climb down from here and pick up de supplies we left on de sand dune yesterday," Reggie said.

"Okay," Wendell moaned as he slid down the trunk of the tree and headed towards the beach. "It's only been three days since the crash and I need some rest." Rolling on his back after they retrieved their supplies, he allowed the early morning breeze to soothe his tortured body and closed his eyes.

"We need ta get something ta eat first," Reggie announced and began to unpack his gear. "We can sleep after breakfast; den we can set up camp." Picking up a jug of water, he took several swallows and passed it over to Wendell.

"Are you kidding?" Opening his eyes, Wendell took a long swig of water, placed the cap back on the jug and said, "I'd rather get some sleep. I'm too tired to chase fish."

"Suit yourself," Reggie shrugged and stripped down to his shorts before gathering up his snorkeling gear. "When you wake up hungry don't expect me ta go back out again and catch breakfast fer you."

"What a sport," Wendell grimaced as he grudgingly got up.

"Have you ever snorkeled before?" Reggie asked.

"No, but I don't suppose it's that hard."

"Good to hear dat. Strip down ta your shorts and follow me. I've brought some extra gear. Before we head out, I want ta make sure you know how ta use it."

Sitting on the arched trunk of a palm tree, Reggie laid out his snorkeling equipment and explained to Wendell how to tighten the facemask strap and use the flippers and snorkel. "Be sure dat you always spit inta de mask and rub it all over de inside of de glass before you go inta de water. Den rinse de mask out with seawater. Dat'll prevent de glass from fogging up."

Wendell took the snorkeling equipment and reluctantly began putting it on. "What about the flippers? Should I put them on now or wait until I'm in the water?'

"Wait; I'd hate ta see you trip over dem."

Picking up the flippers, Wendell headed down the beach, waded into the shallow water, sat down, and slipped the flippers on.

"How do dey feel?" Reggie asked.

"All right, I guess."

"Good. I was hoping dey'd fit. Dey'll make swimming a lot easier."

"I've been noticing the spear you're taking with you. What's it called?" Wendell asked.

"A Hawaiian sling. My father made it fer me."

"Are you good at catching fish with it?"

"De best," Reggie smiled proudly.

"Well, if I'm supposed to help you catch fish, do you have an extra one that I could use?"

"Yeah, but it takes lots of practice ta learn ta use it. For now, your job is ta help me spot fish. We're headed ta a coral reef I located earlier. When we swim out, stay as close ta me as possible so I don't lose track of you."

As they swam out, Wendell had some problems breathing through the snorkel as he tried to follow Reggie. He didn't like the gurgling sounds, and several times he sucked seawater into his snorkel and swallowed a mouthful. Tugging at Reggie's flipper, he motioned him to stop.

"You're going too fast," Wendell gasped after he and Reggie stuck their heads above water and removed their mouthpieces. "I keep swallowing seawater and I don't like the gurgling sounds."

"You've got water trapped in your snorkel," Reggie sputtered. "Take a deep breath and blow air through de snorkel. Dat'll clear de water out and take away de gurgling sound. It would also help if you didn't swim with your head so far beneath de surface. Dat's why you're sucking in sea water."

"Ugh," Wendell belched, "I think I'm going to vomit."

"I'm not surprised. Swallowing seawater can do dat ta you. Just try ta relax and breathe slowly. De reef is only a short distance away."

After clearing his snorkel and waiting a moment to get his stomach under control, Wendell stuck his face beneath the surface and spotted the huge coral mass Reggie was headed towards. At first, the coral and schools of fish appeared as fuzzy images, but as they drew closer, Wendell became mesmerized by the spectacular beauty of this underwater garden. Streaking schools of red, yellow, and green fish swam past in breathtaking ribbons of life, while iridescent clusters of squid darted amongst the shifting shadows. Between the coral boulders, majestic purple and green sea fans swayed to and fro and fleet-footed crabs scurried amongst rocky crevices. He was immersed in a fairyland of dancing colors and the crackling and chomping sounds of snapping shrimp and hungry parrotfish.

Enthralled by the beauty that surrounded him, it wasn't until Reggie tugged Wendell's flipper and pointed with his spear that he noticed the large, mottled fish lurking in the shadows. Using his hands to signal his intent, Reggie dove towards the grouper. The frontal assault briefly paralyzed the animal before it bolted to safety, and Reggie's spear harmlessly zipped past its head. As they swam further through the coral garden, Wendell pointed out several more of the mottled fish but each time Reggie's attempt to spear them failed. *Perhaps Reggie wasn't as good with the spear as he said he was,* Wendell thought to himself. Finally, Reggie's spear rendered a lethal blow. Dark blood poured from the mortally wounded creature as it attempted to get away. Swimming after his catch, Reggie dragged the speared fish away from the reef and motioned Wendell to swim over to meet him.

"What kind of fish is it?" Wendell excitedly asked Reggie when they surfaced alongside one another.

"A Nassau grouper," Reggie announced proudly. "We won't have ta hunt fer anymore food 'til tomorrow. Let's head back. I don't like being out here with an injured fish on de end of my spear. It could attract sharks."

The mere mention of sharks sent tremors of fear racing through Wendell. Without looking to see if any were nearby, he panicked and started swimming towards the beach. Surprised by Wendell's reaction, Reggie lifted his head above the water and yelled for him to slow down, but it was useless. Wendell was too terrified to hear anything. When he reached the beach, he tore off his flippers and facemask and flung himself onto the beach, trying to drive away the images of the sharks tearing into the pilot's body.

"You've got ta get a hold of yourself, Mon," Reggie panted when he caught up with Wendell and looked into his fear-glazed eyes. "Der were no sharks out der. I just wanted ta caution you about dem."

"I know," Wendell sobbed trying to catch his breath, "but I have nightmares about the crash and what happened to the pilot. When I heard you say 'sharks' I panicked. I was sure one of them would come after us when they smelled the fish's blood."

"I'm sorry," Reggie said as he squeezed Wendell's shoulder. "I didn't mean ta frighten you. Try ta relax while I prepare de fish fer breakfast."

"Ok, but I don't think I'll ever be able to sleep again without dreaming of the shark attacks."

Reggie understood because he still had similar nightmares about the death of his parents.

CHAPTER

Early Morning on Lucian Cay

Simone hadn't eaten for over twelve hours. Grief had replaced her desire for food. The apparent death of her father and her failure to find her mother and brother in the cave made her situation seem hopeless. She had no idea how she was going to survive. Turning herself over to the police didn't seem wise. Their brutal treatment of her father was something she never expected. There was no telling what would happen if she placed herself in their hands.

Squeezing out the cave entrance, Simone cautiously swam toward the beach. No one was in sight when she reached the shore. The rafts were gone and all she found were the remnants of the makeshift camp the refugees had set up. Perhaps others had escaped and were hiding nearby.

"Is anyone here?" Simone cried out.

A comfortable northeasterly breeze blowing through the palm fronds and the pounding of surf against the shore were the only sounds she heard. Once again, she yelled out. Once again, no one answered. It's no use, she thought. Collapsing onto the sand, she began to cry.

An unexpected shuffling of feet in the sand caused Simone to lift her head and wipe the tears from her face. Standing between her and the early morning sun, a stranger cast a thin, cool shadow over her body.

"You called?" a raspy voice replied.

It wasn't a voice she recognized. Turning around, she shielded her eyes and stared at the silhouette of the nameless stranger.

"I won't hurt you," he promised.

"W-who are you?" Simone stammered. "Are you Haitian?"

"I am," the man acknowledged. "My name is Daniel."

"Were you on the boat with us?" Simone asked before standing up to get a better look at him.

Shifting his eyes away from her appraising stare, the Haitian paused a moment before answering. "No." The foul odor of his rotting teeth made Simone take a step backwards. "I'm living with some of our people on the north end of Fortune Island. Our leader is a priest. He sent me to see if anyone else escaped the police raid."

"Then you found some of the others?" a hopeful Simone asked.

"Yes," Daniel acknowledged. "I'm happy to report that quite a few people avoided being captured."

"Where are they?"

"We took them to Fortune Island. They were pretty frightened and hungry when we rescued them."

"Did you find a woman by the name of Marie and a young boy named Michael?"

Daniel rubbed the gray stubble on the end of his wrinkled chin. "We might have. If my memory serves me, there was a boy about eight or nine. I think someone else found him hiding in the underbrush with his mother."

"That could be them," Simone said excitedly. "Are they all right?"

"Except for a few minor cuts and bruises, they appeared to be okay."

"Thank God," Simone sighed. "What about a tall man? Six foot one wearing a floral print shirt? He's my father. He was shot when the police raided the camp."

"No, I'm sorry. They must of have taken him away."

"He was injured pretty badly. I pray he's still alive."

Daniel placed a consoling hand on Simone's shoulder. "I hope so too, but you can't stay here. The police will soon be back to see if they can find anyone else. My boat is just up the beach. I can take you to our camp. I'm sure your mother and brother are there and will be happy to see you."

Simone didn't know whether or not to trust the stranger but under the circumstances she had no choice. She needed to locate the rest of her family and find out if they were okay. "How far away is your camp?" she asked.

"Less than a half hour by boat."

"That's pretty far."

"Not as far as you think," Daniel smiled, sensing the girl's reluctance. "If you look across the water you can see Fortune Island from here."

Turning around, Simone scanned the horizon and located the sliver of land he was referring to. "You're right. It's not that far. I guess we should get going before the police return."

Nodding his head, Daniel led Simone to his boat and helped her on board. He was certain the priest would reward him handsomely for finding her. Perhaps he would even give him one of the young women they had captured earlier. Casting an admiring glance at Simone, Daniel watched his attractive young passenger clutch a cloth sack she was wearing around her neck and smiled.

CHAPTER

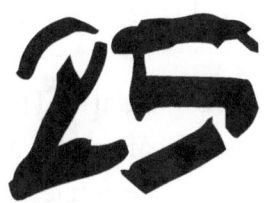

Colonel Hill Police Station, Crooked Island, Day Three

"I still have nothing ta report about your son," the police chief said as he looked across his desk at Wendell's distraught parents. They had arrived the previous day and had asked to meet with him. "We've found de wreckage of de plane about a half mile from Goat Cay. Divers from de airline company have gone over it pretty thoroughly but haven't recovered anyone. Dey also reported dat de plane's life raft was missing. It's possible de pilot and your son used it ta get ta one of de nearby islands. Other dan de wreckage, de only thing aerial spotters found was a group of Haitian refugees. My guess is dey were set adrift by an unscrupulous captain who abandoned dem after he stole all der money. De police in Nassau have been notified and are sending some boats ta pick dem up.

Tomorrow, my assistant and I are going out again with some fishermen ta conduct a more thorough search of some islands near de place de plane went down."

"We'd like to go with you," Ben said anxiously as he placed a comforting arm around his wife. "I'm sure you can use the extra help."

"Normally, I wouldn't do dat." The police chief paused briefly. "But in your case, I can make an exception. I'm also going ta take Lewis Garland, de uncle of a local boy who ran away from home recently. He's organized a search party of fishermen ta help find his nephew. If we're lucky we might locate both of dem. I intend ta leave from de Landrail pier at 7:30 in de morning."

"We heard about Lewis' nephew. It will be nice to see Lewis again. I grew up on the island and went to school with the boy's father," Emily Jenkins said. "I was also sorry to hear about the tragic deaths of Lewis' sister and her husband."

"We all were," the police chief sighed. "Dey were outstanding members of our community. We all sang together in de church choir."

"Thanks for letting us go with you and keeping us informed," Ben said. "We'll be there in the morning."

"I'm sure I'd want ta be part of de search party if dis had happened ta my son. I understand you're staying with your father, Mrs. Jenkins," the chief added.

"Yes."

"Your father has been over here a couple times since de crash, and he's joined de fishermen's search team. He's very worried. I'm sure you've been a great comfort ta each other."

Standing, the chief went to the door with Wendell's parents. Once outside the building, he watched them walk along the puddle-filled road back to Wendell's grandfather's house. *They're a nice couple,* he thought as he reentered the police station. He simply didn't have the heart to tell them everything he knew. Yesterday, a sport fisherman caught a large bull shark with the partial remains of a human inside its stomach. The body parts were sent to a lab in Nassau to see if they could be identified, but after looking at some of the undigested pieces of clothing, he was almost certain that they belonged to the pilot.

CHAPTER

26

Japapa's Camp, North End of Fortune Island

"Where do you think my mother and brother are?" Simone questioned Daniel while she looked over at the bedraggled people wandering around the Haitian camp on Fortune Island. "I don't recognize anyone from our group."

"I'm not surprised." Daniel grinned. "The people we rescued yesterday are setting up camp on the other side of the island. I'm sure our leader will help you get in touch with them. Come, I'll introduce you."

"Thanks." Simone smiled timidly and followed Daniel inland.

As they moved through the rest of the camp, Simone was troubled by what she saw. There were very few women, and the men's leering glances made her feel extremely uncomfortable.

After passing several poorly constructed shelters along the path, Simone turned towards Daniel and asked how long the camp had been there.

"Not long," Daniel answered. Walking slowly, they made their way up a rain-soaked surface of a narrow trail to the top of the hill. "I only arrived a week ago. When I came to the Bahamas from Jamaica, I hoped to find a job in the islands but things didn't pan out. I couldn't get a work permit so I tried to sneak into the United States. I had some friends living in Miami and felt sure if I could get there they'd help me find a job and give me a place to stay."

"What happened?"

"I never made it. There were four of us who pooled our money to pay for the trip. We gave it to a fisherman who promised he could get us there. When we were about an hour west of Andros, he set us adrift in a raft with practically no food or water. We floated around the ocean for nearly nine days before someone from this camp rescued us. Another fellow and I were the only ones to survive. We managed to do it by eating raw fish and drinking rainwater."

"Almost the same thing happened to us." Simone sighed and shook her head. "It's hard to believe people can be that cruel." Anxiously looking around, she turned and asked Daniel how much further.

"We're almost there. Our leader is near the top of the hill. In fact, I can see him from here. He's standing underneath that large gumbo limbo tree."

Shielding her eyes from the sun, Simone spotted a tall, obese figure waving his fist in the air. Thick layers of sweaty flesh slapped against the Haitian's side as his angry baritone voice smothered the men standing in front of him with dread.

"We better wait here," Daniel cautioned. "I don't think it would be wise to interrupt him now."

"I want those supplies before nightfall!" the priest demanded. Smashing his fist into the palm of his hand, he scowled at one of the men who groveled before him. "If you don't get them, I'll slit you open and feed your liver to the dogs."

"But we don't know where they are, my Lord." The trembling man's eyes remained fixed on the ground. "One of the locals told us where he thought the plane went down, but we weren't able to find it."

Reaching out, the leader lifted the man off his feet and stared into eyes. "Are you telling me that you gave up without looking any further?" he snarled.

"Y-yes, my Lord," the terrified man stammered before the priest tossed him back to the ground. "He appeared to be the only one who seemed to know anything." The Haitian trembled with fear at the feet of the irate priest.

"I can't believe there wasn't someone else who knew something," the priest growled. I should have you horsewhipped for being so stupid. Now get out of my sight, you sniveling bunch of lizards. And don't come back until you've found those supplies." Picking their spokesperson up off the ground, the men quickly retreated down the hill. "Hurry up, you fools," the priest yelled, "or I'll make sure that all of you are fed to the buzzards." Another round of laughter followed before the camp leader abruptly turned and glared at Daniel and snarled, "And what do you want?"

"My Lord, I would like to introduce you to Simone Joseph. I found her on Lucian Cay. She's part of that group we found earlier. She thinks her mother and younger brother might be here."

A broad toothy smile replaced the priest's angry demeanor. "I see. I hope I didn't frighten you with that outburst. I sent those men to retrieve medical supplies and they let me down. I can't tolerate incompetence. I desperately need those supplies to help my people."

"I-I understand," Simone stammered while she tried to prevent her knees from shaking. "I wonder if you could help me find my mother and younger brother. My mom's name is Marie. She was wearing a plaid blouse. My brother's name is Michael. He's nine and was wearing a yellow t-shirt."

Using his thick forearm to wipe the sweat away from his brow, the priest took a moment to reflect.

"I believe they're part of a work party that I sent out this morning to collect food and set up camp on the other side of the island. They should still be over there. I'll have one of my assistants take you over."

"That would be great." Simone let out a huge sigh of relief. "I'm anxious to catch up with them. I'm hoping they can tell me what happened to my father."

"Of course." The priest motioned to a tall, thin man standing several feet away. This is Peter, my most trusted assistant. He'll help you locate your family. Perhaps after you've gotten together, you'll join me at a celebration feast I'm having this evening."

"What kind of celebration?" Simone asked.

"Tonight, I intend to pay tribute to our gods for allowing us to find and rescue some of your people from the police," the smiling priest proudly announced as he gently placed his massive hand on Simone's shoulder. "It appears your rescue and being able to reunite you with your family is an additional thing to thank them for."

"I'm sure my family and I would be happy to join you," Simone said warily while looking up into the man's face.

"Good. Now that that's settled, I need to speak to someone about some urgent business." After giving Simone's shoulder another friendly squeeze, the priest turned and headed toward his hut.

Once Japapa stepped inside his hut, Peter motioned Simone to follow him.

It took all of Simone's energy to keep up with the priest's lanky assistant. "This path leads to the other side of the island," Peter said as he rapidly moved off in front of her. Tripping over vines and jagged rocks, Simone frequently had to stop and ask Peter to slow down. "I need to rest," she panted before taking a moment to collapse onto a fallen tree trunk.

"We must hurry," Peter implored. Returning to the spot where Simone was resting, he bent over to offer her assistance. "I have other business to attend to today. Give me your hand and I'll help you over the log."

Waving Peter's hand away, Simone panted, "I just need a moment to regain my breath," Simone gasped and pleaded.

"All right, but just a couple of minutes. We're almost there."

"Thanks." Taking some time to look around at the stark landscape, she wondered how they raised crops. "Do you grow any food on the island?" she asked.

"Yes, mostly tomatoes, peppers and eggplant which grow best here during the winter months. Your family may help us harvest some of these vegetables after they finish setting up camp. We must catch up with them soon if I'm going to get back to make arrangements for this evening's celebration." Reaching out and taking hold of Simone's hand, Peter groaned when he tried to pull her up.

"What's wrong?" Simone asked.

"It's nothing," Peter grimaced. "I was working on one of the boats the other day and cut my hand."

But Simone could see otherwise. Human teeth made the wound. A wave of fear swept through her. Suddenly, she suspected it wasn't the police that had carried out the raid but some of the priest's thugs. Turning her head, she tried to avoid the sinister smile on Peter's face as he hurried her along.

Inside Japapa's Hut

Two eyes glared at Japapa as he stepped inside his hut. "I was wondering when you'd show up," the priest grumbled as he put a sweaty rag to his to nose to suppress the odor coming from the creature that stood in a darkened corner of the hut. "It's interesting you've chosen to assume the form of a pig."

"I thought you'd enjoy it," the creature snorted. "I thought it would remind you of me when we worked together in Haiti."

"It's not one of your most endearing life forms," Japapa grumbled.

"I suppose," Baka snorted. "Nevertheless, I came as soon as I could. I'm afraid I've encountered some unwanted visitors."

"Who?" Japapa snarled.

"Two teenage boys. One is the survivor of the plane crash off Goat Cay. The other is a local boy who's run away from home, Reggie Sands. Do you remember that name? He's the son of the couple you had killed in a car crash on Nassau. Now the boy is threatening to come back and haunt you. It appears he wants to move into the plantation house."

"Get rid of both of them," Japapa snarled as he looked anxiously across the hut into the spirit's fierce red eyes. "I don't like the idea of having them around—especially the Sands kid."

"Understood. I doubt I'll have any trouble dealing with these two frail young mortals."

"And what about the hermit who moved to the south end of Fortune Island a year ago. Is he still there?"

"Yes, but he's not a problem. He stays mostly to himself and spends his time fishing for grouper and lobsters."

"Good. Now that you're here, I have an issue of great importance to talk to you about."

"Is it about the girl—Simone?"

"Yes." Japapa frowned and started to pace back and forth.

"You must be cautious about your dealings with her. The high priestess, Mama Atabei, could be using the girl to set a trap."

"That's why I sent for you. I've been seeing the priestess in my dreams. She's been taunting me. The captain of the ship informed me that he's sure he saw the old woman with Simone on the boat. I have no doubt she's waiting for the right moment to get her revenge. I can't let that happen. Now that I've made a fortune smuggling drugs, I intend to return to Haiti as soon as possible. When I do, I'll use the money to buy off local politicians and get myself elected president. However, there are still some people who remember me and some of the things I did to them and their families. I can't let these people ruin my plans. Somehow, I need to regain their trust. I believe I can do this by returning with Simone Joseph as my bride. Not only will this complete my revenge against her father, but people will think Mr. Joseph has become one of my supporters."

"An interesting scheme, but isn't she a little young for you?"

"I'm thirty-eight and she's almost fifteen. Arranged marriages between older men and young girls have often been made for political purposes," Japapa observed.

"That was true in the past, but you don't see too many marriages like that today," Baka cautioned. "And what about the parents and younger brother? How will you deal with them?"

"Joseph's already been taken care of. According to my men, he was killed during the raid on Lucian Cay. The mother and son have escaped, but it won't take me too long to find them and make sure they're no longer a problem. Now, all I need to do is make sure the old priestess doesn't use her powers to upset things. That's where I'll need your help."

"Aren't you strong enough to overcome her magic? If I remember correctly you told me in Haiti that her powers were no match for yours."

"I was young and foolish when I said that. I've since learned to be more cautious. I should have paid more attention to your warning when I left Port-au-Prince. I didn't realize the priestess might still become a problem."

"Your humility is touching. Dealing with the priestess on the other hand is a serious problem; nevertheless, it's one I'm sure I can take care of. My powers are far greater than hers. If you remember, your people summoned me once before to liberate them from the French in Haiti. But, I'll only agree to help you under one condition."

"What's that?" Japapa stopped pacing back and forth and squinted suspiciously at Baka.

"That I rule alongside you when you return to Haiti."

"Hmm." Tapping his fingers against his chin, Japapa took a moment to think about Baka's proposition. It was not an idea he was anxious to accept. However, if his plan were to succeed, he would have to agree to the demon's proposal. Later, he could figure out a way to escape the trap that Baka was trying to set for him. "Your request has merit." Japapa smiled with a sinister grin of apparent satisfaction. "With you by my side, I will again become one of the most powerful people in the world. You could help me maintain my drug smuggling operation in the Bahamas and I could use those funds to maintain my status as Haiti's president. Like before, people will tremble at the mere mention of my name, and the wealth I will accrue will make me invincible."

"A very wise decision," Baka chuckled as he faded into the darkness. The demon knew Japapa never intended to honor their agreement.

CHAPTER

South End of Fortune Island

"That smells awfully good." Sharkman grinned and stepped into the clearing where Reggie and Wendell were cooking breakfast. "It looks like you speared quite a large grouper."

Standing up, Reggie stammered, "W-who are you?" He eyed the scraggly, bearded, old man with suspicion. "I didn't know der was anyone else living on dis island."

"People call me Sharkman. I settled here about a year ago. When I saw your boat sail into the lagoon, I thought I'd pay you a visit. If you don't mind my asking, what brings you to this place?"

"We're thinking about moving into de old plantation house," Reggie said as he invited Sharkman to sit down. "I'm Victor and dis is my cousin Luke. He's from de States," Reggie lied as Wendell rolled his eyes and shook his head.

"Pleased to meet you." Sharkman smiled and looked over at the reaction on Wendell's face. He was certain the young men were the ones everybody was looking for. He had heard about the plane accident and the fact that a boy had run away from the home of a local fisherman. The real question was what were the two of them doing together. "I'm afraid it's too late to move into the plantation house," Sharkman sighed. "Baka has already moved in."

"Who's Baka?" Wendell asked.

"A demon in the form of a pig. He's named after the evil spirit the Haitians called upon to drive the French colonialists from their country."

"We've already run inta him," Reggie grumbled as he shook his head and flipped the fish over in the fire. "He chased us up a tree yesterday when we went ta look at de house. I've been thinking all morning about ways dat I can get rid of him."

"Baka's mean," the agitated parrot squawked as it bobbed its head up and down on Sharkman's shoulder. "Beware of Baka."

"My companion offers good advice." Sharkman frowned and handed the bird a sea grape from his pocket. "I would be very careful about how I dealt with Baka. He possesses very powerful magic."

"You don't have ta worry. I don't believe in evil spirits and I've handled pigs before," Reggie boasted. "Dey are not hard ta get rid of when you know how ta go about it."

Surprised by Reggie's smug response, Sharkman nodded his head and smiled. "I wouldn't be so sure. He's extremely cunning, and there're lots of people who have observed his supernatural powers. He's also very strong. I can testify to that. Several wild dogs on the island cornered him once. I heard them battling Baka on the beach, and by the time I arrived to see what all the ruckus was about, he'd killed every one."

"Dos dogs were stupid," Reggie scoffed and leaned over to check the fish. "I don't intend ta get dat close ta him. How about something ta eat?" Removing one of the fish filets from the fire, Reggie placed it on a bed of sea grape leaves and offered it to Sharkman. "We've got plenty."

"Thanks." Sharkman reached out and cradled the leaf in his hand. Once it cooled, he began eating the fish with his fingers.

"Are der any other people living on de island?" Reggie asked after removing another filet from the fire and giving it to Wendell.

"Yes, that's another thing I wanted to warn you about. There's a band of Haitian pirates and drug smugglers that have settled on the north end. They're a mean bunch and won't hesitate to slit your throat if they catch you snooping around their camp. Their leader is called Japapa. He claims he's a voodoo priest who was head of the secret police for one of the former Haitian presidents. When the president was overthrown, he and some of his followers fled to the Bahamas. They moved onto the north end of Fortune Island just after I got here."

Wendell stopped eating and gave Sharkman a concerned look. "Why don't the police do something about them?" he asked.

"They've tried to catch them a few times. But they're clever. They always seem to know ahead of time when the police are coming. Just the other day, I overheard a couple of them laughing and boasting in the woods about how their priest paid informants to let him know whenever there was going to be a raid on their camp. Once he got wind of an attack, he divided his band of cutthroats into small groups and had them slip away under the cover of darkness. By the time the police got tired of chasing them, they would regroup on one of the other islands in the area. A couple of months ago, they decided to settle on the north end of this one. I'm sure the police know they're here. It's just a matter of capturing them."

"Do dey come down ta dis end often?" Reggie asked.

"Not often. I've only seen them twice. Both times there were only two or three of them. As far as I could tell, they were scouting out places where they could harvest conch."

"Well, we'll certainly keep an eye out fer dem," Reggie said as he stood up and offered Sharkman another filet. "You're just full of good news. Is der anything else you want ta pass along?"

"Yes." Sharkman nodded and waved away Reggie's second portion of fish. "And in some ways it frightens me more than Baka and Japapa's band of cutthroats."

"What's dat?" Reggie asked.

"It's the *Chogers.*"

After taking a second helping of fish from Reggie, Wendell remembered his dream aboard the plane and wondered if these were the same creatures in his nightmare. "What are *Chogers?*" he asked.

"Dey are ghosts," Reggie said nervously, "evil spirits dat roam about whenever de mist rises from de ocean."

"Have you ever seen them?" Wendell asked.

"No, but my father said he knew a man who was killed by dem. His wife said dey came through de window of der house at night and choked him ta death when he was asleep. She said dey also tried ta kill her but she managed ta escape."

"*Chogers* kill!" the parrot squawked and flapped its wings. "Beware of *Chogers*."

"W-why do you think there are *Chogers* on this island?" Wendell stammered. "My father says there are no such things as ghosts. They're just make-believe."

"I used to think that too," Sharkman agreed as he gave his parrot another piece of fruit to calm him down. "Since I've moved to the islands, now I'm not so sure. Too many people have disappeared and too many unusual things have happened for me not to believe in them."

"I don't believe der are any on dis island. You're just trying ta frighten us so we'll leave," Reggie replied with a nervous laugh.

"Believe what you like." Sharkman shrugged his shoulders. "I'm fairly certain they exist, and if you intend to live here, you must be prepared to deal with them. Already, there are warning signs that they are coming."

"What kind of signs?" Wendell asked.

"Bubbles. Whenever you see them rising to the surface of the ocean, it's not too long before the ocean becomes shrouded in a fog-like mist and people begin to die."

"H-how come they haven't killed you?" Wendell stammered.

"I know better than to ignore the warning signs. Whenever I see them, I take off. I suggest you do the same."

"Well, dey won't get us. I'll make sure of dat," Reggie challenged. "Once we kill Baka, we'll fix de house up so nothing can get us."

"I see," Sharkman replied. "I guess it's time for me to leave. Thanks for the fish. If I were you, I'd fix up that house as soon as possible and pay very close attention to the bubbles offshore. I'm beginning to see more of them every day, and I'm thinking about finding another place to move to. You might be safe in the house if you seal it off properly. However, some people have been found dead in their homes even though their doors were locked and the windows closed."

CHAPTER

Landrail, Crooked Island

Emily Jenkins shook Lewis Garland's hand as she boarded the patrol boat and it pulled away from the Landrail pier. "I'm glad you could join us. You know, I went to school with your younger sister. I was shocked when my father told me about the car accident. It must have been hard on everyone."

"It was," Lewis acknowledged, "especially fer my nephew Reggie. He idolized his father. After de death of his parents, I thought it would be best if he went ta Nassau ta live with my older sister and her husband. We didn't have room fer him at our house. I never thought he'd run away. Looking back, I guess de decision ta send him away ta live with his aunt wasn't such a good idea."

Emily shook her head in agreement and wiped a tear away from the corner of her eye. "I thought it would be a good idea to send our son to Crooked Island to visit his grandfather during the Christmas holiday. I have lots of fond memories of this place and thought Wendell would really enjoy spending some time fishing and exploring new places with him. Now I regret encouraging him to go."

"Mistakes are part of life. We all learn by dem. I just hope de ones we've made won't come back ta haunt us," Lewis responded.

"We're headed ta Goat Cay," the police chief hollered so that Lewis and the Jenkins could hear him above the roar of the boat's engines. "It's near de site where Wendell's plane went down. A group of scientists just set up camp der yesterday. While we're unloading de supplies dey wanted, I'll try ta find out if dey spotted anything unusual. Dey may even be willing ta help us search de island fer some clues."

Grabbing his hat so it wouldn't fly away, Ben Jenkins asked the chief, "What are the scientists doing on the island?"

"Geology work for de government, but a lot of de local people don't believe dat. Dey think dey are studying de Bermuda Triangle."

"Do you believe the Bermuda Triangle exists?" Emily inquired as their boat veered to the southwest.

"No, not really. But I do know dat der work has something ta do with gas escaping from de ocean floor. Dey've spent a lot of time talking ta local fishermen about de bubbles dey've seen rising ta de surface."

"I remember dem," Lewis Garland said. "Dey stopped by my house several days ago. Dey had me point out where I'd seen de bubbles on a map. Dey seemed pleased with de information I gave dem."

"Well, I hope they know something that will help us find Wendell and Reggie." Emily scanned the horizon anxious to spot Goat Cay and sighed. "How much longer before we get there?"

"About thirty minutes," the chief said as he watched the tension on his passengers' faces mount and prayed that the scientists would be able to provide some valuable information.

CHAPTER

The Waters North of Lucian Cay

There was a terrible pain in his right shoulder. "Where are we?" Claude Joseph moaned as he opened his eyes.

"Aboard a raft." A look of concern spread across Marie's face when she looked down at her husband. "You've lost a lot of blood. Don't move around so much."

"What about the children?"

"Michael's here." Marie sobbed and shook her head.

"And Simone?"

"I don't know." Marie wiped the tears from her face. "There was a lot of confusion during the attack."

"Were they police?"

"No. I overheard some of them shouting to one another during the raid. They were drug smugglers from Fortune Island. Their leader is your former enemy—the priest, Japapa. It appears our boat captain told the priest where we were before he set us adrift. They captured many of the women and seemed especially interested in locating you and Simone. Most of the men died in the battle, and after they shot you and left you for dead, they went after Simone."

"I remember pleading with her to escape. Did she get away?"

"I think so. The last I saw her; she was headed towards the ocean. When I saw that you were shot, I went back to see if I could help. But before I got to you, one of the men from the boat grabbed me by the arm and said it wouldn't be safe. He dragged Michael and me into the bushes. We stayed there until the raiding party left. After they were gone, Michael and I ran down to check on you. You were unconscious and had lost a lot of blood. Fortunately, one of the men that survived had medical training and was able to patch you up. After I saw that you would be ok, I tried to find the cave you talked about, but the others said we had to leave. They were afraid that a Bahamian patrol boat would find us, or some of Japapa's men would come back to see if anyone else was left on the island. We were lucky. They left a few of the rafts behind and we were able to use them to escape."

"We've got to find our daughter!" Claude pleaded. "I hate to think what will happen if Japapa captures her. She's probably hiding in the cave, too frightened to come out. If we go back, I might be able to rescue her."

"We can't go back." Marie gently forced her husband to lie down when he tried to sit up. "You'd never survive the trip. We're headed north to a populated island. Everyone says we'll be safer there and we might be able to find medical help for you and some of the other injured people."

Lowering his body, Claude gave a sigh of frustration as he watched the puffy clouds pass overhead. He knew their effort to find a safe place to live was coming to an end.

CHAPTER

Near the Ruins of the Plantation House, South End of Fortune Island

Hiding behind some bushes, Reggie and Wendell waited for Baka to make his appearance. "I don't understand why he doesn't leave," Reggie complained. "Boars usually take off when humans move in, but dis one is stubborn. De piss we spread around de house didn't scare him off. Neither did all de loud noises we created. Now we have no choice but ta kill him."

"I think you're nuts," Wendell grumbled. Nervously scanning the trail, Reggie and Wendell looked for signs of movement. "Why don't we just let him have this broken down building and build your home someplace else?"

"Because I don't want ta live someplace else. Der's no way I'm going ta let dat dumb animal drive me away from dis place. Dis is where my father wanted our family ta live and dis is where I'm going ta stay."

"Great," Wendell moaned, "I always wanted to die young pursuing someone else's dream. I hate to tell you but I'm afraid we don't stand a chance in hell of killing a demon in the form of a wild boar with these homemade spears you've put together. I've seen rotten tree limbs that were a lot sturdier. Why don't we kill him with the spear from the Hawaiian sling? This animal is huge. If we nick him and he gets angry, he could turn us both into hamburger meat."

"Take it from me, Mon, dat's not going ta happen." Reggie pursed his lips and shook his head defiantly. "Dese spears are stronger dan you think. My father showed me how ta make 'em. One stab in de heart and it's all over."

"Swell," Wendell responded sarcastically. "I'm just not sure which of us will be alive after the attack—the pig or us."

Since there was no way to change Reggie's mind, Wendell stopped arguing and waited for the animal to show up. The site they had chosen for the ambush was one Baka took regularly to reach his favorite feeding ground. Reggie had scouted it out and decided it would be the perfect place for their sneak attack. It had plenty of cover, and it was downwind from where they expected the creature to show up.

"I can smell him," Reggie whispered. With sweat forming on his brow, he tightened his grip on the spear and waited. "It won't be long now."

"Swell," Wendell grumbled, "you can't imagine how confident that makes me feel."

"Der! Can you see him?" Reggie asked. "Something just moved behind dat cluster of palms."

With that, the two hundred pound animal emerged from the thick palms and began sniffing the air and trotting out into the open. The air was saturated with his strong, musky odor, and his razor-sharp tusks glistened in the early morning sun. Five feet from where Reggie and Wendell were hiding, he stopped, lifted his head and pawed the ground.

"Now!" Reggie shouted. Leaping in front of the boar, he hurled his spear at the astonished beast. There was a loud thud as the weapon glanced off the animal's shoulder and fell harmlessly to the ground. Wendell's spear followed. Streaking through the air, it penetrated deep into the animal's rump. Blood spurted from the wound as Baka squealed and began running in circles and gnashing his teeth.

"Let's get out of here!" Wendell yelled. Grabbing Reggie's shirtsleeve, he tried to encourage the Bahamian to run. "He's going to kill us!"

The animal's anguished cries sent waves of fear running down Wendell's spine. If they didn't get out of here now, he was certain they would die.

"No. Wait!" Reggie shouted. Suddenly, the creature stopped running in circles and bolted into the bushes. "You hurt him pretty bad. Look at all de blood on de ground. We can follow de trail and finish him off."

"Are you crazy?" Wendell said in astonishment. "When we catch up with him, he'll be meaner than ever. And if he has the supernatural powers Sharkman said he has, who knows what will happen to us."

"Listen to me, Mon." Reggie reached across and grabbed hold of Wendell's shoulder in an effort to calm him down. "Dat boar isn't going ta attack us. He's looking fer someplace ta hide so he can recover from his wound. All we have ta do is follow de trail of blood. Eventually, he'll lose so much blood it'll be easy fer us ta finish him off."

"So, you say. Suppose he isn't as bad off as you think. He could turn around and attack us from the bushes before either one of us can react."

"He won't," Reggie assured Wendell. Without another word, he picked up his spear and proceeded to follow the blood trail left by the animal.

Wendell shook his head in disbelief. "Maybe you believe that, but I don't."

"Okay. Den I'll go after him by myself. And when I finish him off, I'll meet you back on de beach."

"And what happens to me if you get killed? I'm stuck on this island with a crazy old coot who believes in ghosts, one angry pig, and a bunch of drug-smuggling crooks. No thanks! Hand me the other spear you made and we'll go after him together."

"All right!" Reggie grinned and softly jabbed Wendell on his shoulder with his fist.

Stalking the wounded boar wasn't difficult. Small pools of blood led straight to the abandoned house. As they cautiously moved forward, Wendell could feel the sweat dripping off his forehead. With each bend in the trail, his heart pounded with anticipation. He was absolutely certain the creature would be waiting to ambush them. Fortunately, he was wrong.

"Look," Reggie whispered and motioned for Wendell to stop. "It's de end of your spear. It must've broken off when Baka ran through de underbrush. Judging from de amount of blood on de ground, I'd say dat it's cut through an artery. "It's hard fer me ta believe he's run off ta far. I'm willing ta bet he's hiding in dat bush in front of us."

"Swell," Wendell sighed. "How about we forget the whole thing."

"No way, Mon. Dis is our chance ta finish him off."

"Yeah. Or maybe it's his opportunity to turn us into chopped liver."

"Where's your courage, Mon?" Reggie taunted.

"Back on the trail where the beast tried to kill me." Reluctantly following Reggie toward the bush with his spear held high, he stopped and squinted. "Did you see that?" Wendell whispered. "That bush in front of us just moved."

"Yeah, Mon, I saw it ta. Try not ta make any more noise. It won't be long now."

Once again the bushes moved. Each boy tightened the grip on his spear and waited.

"He's coming out!" Wendell nervously whispered.

Before either one of them could throw their spears, two frightened goats scurried out of the bushes and scampered towards the beach.

"Whew, fer a second I thought it was de pig." Reggie loosened his grip on the spear and wiped the sweat from his brow.

"Yeah, me too." Wendell sighed and lowered his weapon. "Do you still think he's hiding in those bushes?"

"I'm sure of it, Mon. De trail of blood runs straight into dem. He's probably close ta dying."

"If that's the case, why don't we just leave him alone? Why take any more chances? Especially if we know he's going to die."

"You're probably right." Reggie said. "It might be a lot safer fer us ta wait him out."

But Baka had different plans. The terrifying sound of gnashing teeth suddenly erupted from the trail behind them. Stunned by the surprise attack, the two boys turned with their mouths agape. Only thirty yards separated them from the charging boar whose red eyes blazed with hatred.

"H-how did he get behind us?" Wendell yelled as the crazed pig raced in their direction.

"I don't' know, Mon," Reggie shouted. Lifting his spear, Reggie hurled it towards the charging beast. Once again his spear missed and skimmed across the back of the hard charging creature. Rooted to the ground, Wendell watched in terrified disbelief.

"Run!"

Before Wendell could react, the two hundred pound boar knocked him to the ground with bone-crushing force. Unable to get up, Wendell lifted his head to look for the animal. A few yards away, it turned, snorted, and got ready to charge again. Saliva dripped from its mouth as it streaked towards him with enraged squeals. Paralyzed with fear, Wendell stared at the boar in disbelief. Baka's impact sent a wave of pain through his body followed by the warm feeling of blood spreading across his chest. Was this what it was like to die? Opening his eyes, he saw the quivering body of the creature lying across his body and the concerned face of Sharkman staring down at him.

"I tried to warn you about Baka but you wouldn't listen." Bending over, Sharkman pulled out the spear and pushed the boar's body off Wendell.

"I know," Wendell groaned and fainted before Sharkman was able to lift him to his feet.

CHAPTER

Japapa's Camp, North End of Fortune Island

What a fool she'd been. Inching her way along the moist cave wall, Simone searched for a way out. What made her think that she could trust these people? Her mother and brother weren't on this island. She so much wanted to believe that they had been rescued that she'd allowed herself to be duped into being captured by the same group of thugs that had attacked her people. Now, what terrible fate awaited her? Judging from the vile grin on Peter's face before he tossed her into the cave, it wasn't good.

"Welcome," a woman's familiar voice called out.

"W-who's there?" Simone stammered as her eyes tried to adjust to the cave's dark interior.

"A friend. Don't you remember me? You saved my life."

"Now I do." Simone sighed with relief. "Did Japapa's men capture you?" she asked when the old woman moved closer.

"No."

"Then how did you get here?"

"If I told you, you wouldn't believe me. But you shouldn't be concerned about that now. I've come to help you. Japapa has plans for your future."

"Japapa! Is he the priest that is in charge of this camp?"

"I'm afraid he is," the woman acknowledged.

"J-just what kind of plans does he have for me?" Simone stammered.

Reaching out, the old woman traced the contours of Simone's face with her gnarled and wrinkled fingers. "I have to admit Japapa's right about you. You are a very beautiful young girl."

Stepping away from the woman, Simone trembled. "Can you help me escape?"

"I believe I can but you mustn't be so impatient," the old woman sighed. "I expect he'll tell you shortly what his plans are. Japapa is a mighty voodoo sorcerer—a *bokor* who uses magic for evil purposes. As you probably know from your father, when Japapa was in Haiti, he did many bad things to your people. Before you were born, your father led an attack on the president's palace forcing Japapa and other corrupt leaders to flee the country. Japapa never forgave him for that."

"How do you know all this?"

"I was there when it happened. Japapa and I are old enemies. Initially, he tried to use his powers of persuasion to get me to join him, but I resisted his efforts. For years, I used my voodoo powers in an effort to destroy him and I almost did. But then, he joined with a powerful force from the underworld to defeat me. When I was in Haiti, his men captured me and placed me on a deserted island. I'd still be there if some of my followers hadn't found me and returned me to Haiti. Now the time has come for me to get my revenge. Soon, I intend to rid the world of this evil man."

"How?"

"I have my ways, but for now, I'm more concerned about you. Japapa has planned for a long time to bring you to these islands. To do so, he has enlisted the help of the evil spirit, *Met Kafou Legba*, the destroyer of life. This spirit has taken control of your destiny."

"I don't believe in voodoo and evil spirits. My father says that there is no way your life can be controlled by such things."

"Believe as you will." The old woman sighed and shook her head. "But you'll see soon enough that what I'm telling you is true. I tried to warn you through your dreams."

"W-what do you mean?" Simone stammered.

"Remember the nightmares you had in Haiti? It was I who created those dreams and gave you a glimpse of the future. I hoped they would serve as a warning and you would avoid being captured. But my magic is too weak to free you from the grip of the *Met Kafou Legba*."

A shaft of white light suddenly streamed into the darkness of the cave as Simone turned her head and shielded her eyes. Standing against the light of the cave's entrance was Japapa's burley silhouette. "I hope you haven't been treated too harshly." The priest's boisterous laughter resounded throughout the lime rock walls. "I'm here to take you to the bridal hut and prepare you for the wedding ceremony."

"What wedding ceremony?" Simone asked as she rubbed her arms and tried to drive away the chill that was seeping into her bones.

"Why, yours of course."

When Simone looked around for the old woman, she had disappeared. She could only hear her faint whispers from the dark recesses of the cave. "Be clever," she said. "Once you find a way to escape, I'll be there to help you."

At the entrance to the cave, a grinning Japapa lumbered towards her. Simone gasped as the salty, rancid smell emanating from his body seeped into her nostrils. Reaching out with his burly hands, Japapa took hold of her arm and pushed her towards the cave entrance. "It's time to go," he said with a sinister chuckle.

CHAPTER

Goat Cay

"Have you seen any signs of a life raft?" the police chief asked the group's lead scientist, Jack Nance, while supplies were being unloaded from his patrol boat.

"No. We've been too busy with our scientific studies. We spent the last couple of days setting up equipment and visiting some of the people on nearby islands. A fisherman told us about the crash. Do you think survivors washed up here?"

"It's a possibility. One of de passengers was a boy named Wendell. His parents are with us. I don't want ta get in de way of what you're doing, but my assistant and I would like ta scout out de island and see if we can spot anything."

"No problem. I'm sure my associates wouldn't mind taking some time out to give you a hand."

"I hoped you'd offer. We need all de help we can get."

"Let me call my team over and you can tell us what you'd like us to do."

After Jack Nance gathered everyone on the beach, the chief introduced himself and told them what he was looking for. "We're trying ta locate a life raft and a thirteen-year-old boy who might have washed up on dis island several days ago. De raft came from de plane dat crashed nearby. I'm sure most of you have heard about de accident. The boy's name is Wendell Jenkins. Dese are his parents. Also joining us on de search is Lewis Garland, de uncle of Reggie Jenkins, a boy who's run away from home. He's hoping dat Reggie might have also stopped by dis island. If dat's true, de boys may have hooked up with one another. I realize everyone is very busy but we could really use your help. Any evidence you could uncover about either of de boys would be greatly appreciated. I'd like you ta work in teams of two. My assistant and I will cover de shore on de far side of de island, and I'd like de rest of you ta cover some of de inland areas and de beaches on dis side. If you spot anything, please notify my assistant or me immediately. We can use our radios ta communicate with each other. Do you have any questions?"

"Shouldn't we be looking for the pilot as well?" someone asked.

"I regret ta say he was killed in de crash. I just received official word dat body parts found in de stomach of a shark caught by a local fisherman off Crooked Island a couple of days ago belonged ta him."

Shocked to hear about the pilot's demise, Emily lifted her hands to her face and stared at her husband in disbelief.

"Is there anything besides the raft we should be looking for?" another scientist asked.

"Pieces of clothing, evidence of a camp site, footprints, any clues dat would reveal dat either of de boys were here," the chief said.

"Do you have any pictures of the boys?"

"We do," the chief replied as his assistant began passing out copies. "Any other questions?"

When there were no more questions, everyone paired up and headed off in different directions.

Wendell's mom joined up with Jan Larsen, a geologist who had just received her doctorate from the University of Texas. Jan was a slender, attractive, young lady with long, blonde hair that was tied up into a bun. Her bubbly, outgoing personality made Emily feel at ease, and the two of them quickly started up a conversation.

"I'm shocked to hear about your son," Jan said after starting their walk down the beach. "Hopefully we'll find the raft and some evidence your son is still alive."

"I hope so." Emily forced a faint smile. "It's been days since the accident and I'm afraid I'm beginning to feel that he may have perished during the crash. The fact that the pilot was eaten by sharks doesn't help."

"You've got to remain optimistic." Stopping, Jan and Emily took a moment to scan the shoreline before proceeding further. "Proof that the raft was missing from the plane should give you some hope."

"I guess," Emily admitted.

"I know how you feel. My family went through a similar situation with my older brother. He was reported missing in Afghanistan. When we first heard the news, I was devastated, but my Dad said I shouldn't lose hope. A few days later, the army informed us he was being held prisoner."

"Did he get home safely?"

"Eventually. It took a while for our troops to rescue him, and he was a bit banged up and a lot skinnier when he got back to the States."

"I hope Wendell will be as lucky as your brother."

"I know he will," Jan replied and tried to give Emily a comforting smile.

"Thanks," Emily nodded thoughtfully before changing the subject. "If you don't mind my asking, is it true that your group is studying the Bermuda Triangle?"

When Emily mentioned the Triangle, Jan tilted her head and laughed. "How quickly rumors spread. Where did you hear that?"

"The police chief mentioned it on our way over."

"Well, I can tell you we're not here to study the Bermuda Triangle. What I can tell you is that the Bahamian government has hired us to study the geology of the ocean bottom at a number of different sites around these islands."

"What about the bubbles?" Emily asked. "Lewis Garland said that you were over to his house asking about places where he saw bubbles rising from the ocean floor."

"That's right. We've been creating a map of the places where gas might be escaping from the ocean bottom. There are some spots, especially underneath the ooze on the continental shelf, where large amounts of methane gas are trapped. The gas comes from the decay of organic life. Sometimes, the gas in these areas slowly escapes to the surface and we get reports from local fishermen and divers about bubbles appearing on the surface."

"Could these bubbles have anything to do with the disappearances that take place within the Triangle?"

After a moment of reflection Jan shook her head. "They could, but I doubt it. However, there are those who believe that the sudden release of large quantities of this gas might be responsible for some of the disappearances that have been reported in the Triangle. Huge oil rigs, for instance, have been known to sink to the bottom of the ocean when a large pocket of methane gas escapes underneath them. When so much gas is released into the water all at once, the density of the sea water is changed and objects floating on the surface sink to the bottom like a rock. In order for that to happen here, I think there would have to be a huge underwater landside along one of the deep troughs next to these islands."

"But it's possible for something like that to happen in this area?"

"Possible, but not likely. There are no reports of any landslides adjacent to the islands we've studied so far. Nevertheless, Crooked Island is within the Bermuda Triangle, and the people who believe that the disappearances are caused by the sudden release of huge amounts of gas suggest that a large earthquake might cause such a landslide. They believe that the earthquakes would take place when the more active

Caribbean plate rubs up against the less active plate that the Bahamas rest on."

"So, according to what these people believe, an earthquake that causes an undersea landslide could release a huge amount of gas which might cause a boat moving across the ocean where this is taking place to sink to the bottom without a trace?"

"Yes."

"But you don't think this could happen in this region of the Bahamas?"

"Correct. I'm a scientist. I'm trained to be skeptical. The main reason we're interested in the gas bubbles is because the people I work for believe the bubbles are coming from small pockets of methane gas on the ocean bottom and that these pockets of gas might become a valuable source of future energy for the Bahamians. That's why we were given the official go-ahead a month ago by the Bahamian government to do exploratory work. However, I don't believe there's enough gas trapped on the bottom in this region to generate the kind of problem some people associate with the Triangle."

"Over here!" one of the scientists exploring the beach suddenly began shouting over his radio. "I think we found the raft covered up with vegetation behind the rocky shoreline."

"It sounds like they've found something," Jan said. Emily's heart began pounding as they raced to the spot where the two scientists were standing. When they arrived, Emily and Jan stopped and stared in horrified disbelief. In front of them was a partially uncovered raft with the decomposed remains of a hand and arm still clinging to its lifeline.

CHAPTER

Sharkman's Hut, South End of Fortune Island

His head was about to be torn off by a gigantic shark. Bolting upright, Wendell shielded his eyes and screamed.

"Danger! Danger!" the terrified parrot squawked before taking flight through the open door of Sharkman's hut.

"There's no reason for you to be frightened." Reaching out, Sharkman rested his hand on Wendell's shoulder and attempted to calm him down. "Baka is dead. I killed him."

"It's not Baka. It's the sharks."

"What sharks?" Sharkman gave Wendell a curious look.

"Those," Wendell sobbed. Using his bruised arm, he brushed aside the old man's hand and pointed towards the roof of the hut.

Looking up, Sharkman quickly realized the reason for Wendell's outburst. Suspended above him were the open jaws of two enormous sharks he'd saved from his shark-fishing days.

"They're horrible." Wendell sobbed. "Why do you keep them? They remind me of the ones that killed the pilot after the plane crashed. If the current hadn't washed me ashore they'd have eaten me."

"When your plane crashed?" Sharkman gave Wendell a suspicious look.

"Yes, I was flying to Crooked Island to stay with my grandpa for Christmas. But we ran into bad weather and the pilot was forced to ditch the plane. I'm Wendell Jenkins. Luke is a name Reggie made up so you wouldn't know who we really are. He said he couldn't take me back to Crooked Island because his uncle would find out where he was and send him to Nassau to live with his aunt. He said after he moved into the plantation house he'd figure out a way to drop me off on Crooked Island without anyone becoming suspicious. I told him he was crazy. People were bound to find out he kidnapped me, but he wouldn't listen. He's possessed by the idea of moving into the plantation house because that's where his family was going to live before they were killed in a car crash."

"I see." Sharkman frowned and shook his head. "Then I suppose your cousin's name really isn't Victor, it's Reggie?"

"Yeah, and we're not related. Can you help me get to Crooked Island? I really miss my folks. By now they must think I'm dead."

"Well, I don't think you'll have to wait much longer. I suspected you were the two boys everyone is looking for. My boat is on the other side of the island. After we get something to eat, I'll make sure you both get back to Landrail."

"Thanks." Wendell gave a sigh of relief. "You don't know how happy that makes me. I didn't know if I'd ever get to see my folks again."

"I can imagine. I'm sure your parents will be equally happy to see you. It's too bad about your shark encounter. I've had a few run-ins with them myself."

"They should all be killed," Wendell grumbled. "No one's safe with them around."

"I understand your feelings, especially after what you've been through, but they're not as terrible as everyone thinks. They play an important role in the marine environment. Killing all of them would upset the balance of nature."

"So, you say. To me, they're nothing but killers. When I was in the raft they turned on their sides and watched me. They were sizing me up waiting for me to fall into the water. When I didn't, one of them began ramming its body into the raft hoping to toss me overboard."

"I see, but that doesn't make them less important to the environment. We often must share our world with creatures we don't like."

"Maybe you do, but I don't." Pulling his knees up against his chest, Wendell stared up at the jaws of the sharks hanging from the ceiling and shivered. "I wouldn't care if every one of them was eliminated."

Sharkman patted Wendell on the knee and stood up. "Time has a way of changing the way you think. Hopefully you'll come to see things differently. Would you like a drink of water?"

"Thanks, my mouth is pretty dry."

Sharkman turned to retrieve some water when Reggie burst into the hut and collapsed to his knees.

"He's gone!" Reggie panted and tried to regain his breath. "Der's not a trace of him. No body—nothin'!"

"Who's gone?" the old man asked as a worried look spread across his face.

"Baka! I went back ta carve him up fer dinner and he'd disappeared. All I found were our broken spears. It's like he never existed."

"I was afraid of this." Sharkman frowned. Heading towards the corner of the hut, the old man began removing some supplies from the shelves and putting some food on the table.

Wendell gave him a curious look and asked him what he meant.

"I told you before that Baka was no ordinary animal. I believe he's a demon whose spirit took possession of that wild boar. Some of Japapa's men probably discovered his body and returned it to their leader. If that's true, I'm certain that Baka's spirit will call upon Japapa to seek revenge for what I did to him."

"How much time do we have before Japapa's men show up?" an astonished Reggie asked.

"Not much. Let's eat and pack some supplies. If we move fast, we can get out of here just after nightfall. I suspect they'll come looking for us first thing in the morning."

CHAPTER

Japapa's Camp, North End of Fortune Island

Japapa's anguished cries could be heard throughout the settlement. No one could sleep, least of all Simone. She kept thinking about the priest's intentions to marry her. The wedding was supposed to take place tomorrow. According to Japapa, the spirits of the afterlife had blessed the event, and as soon as the ceremony was over, he intended to have his followers pay homage to her as a priestess. She found the whole idea revolting. Her only solution was to escape. The trick was figuring out how. "Be clever," was the parting advice the old priestess had given before she stepped back into the dark interior of the cave. That was easy for her to say. She didn't have two guards watching her constantly. After mulling over her options, Simone stuck her head outside the bridal hut and turned to one of them.

"What's the matter with your leader? He's been ranting for hours. It's hard for me to sleep."

"Someone killed Baka," the leaner of the two guards said. A look of concern spread across his face when Japapa cried out again.

"Who's Baka?" Simone asked.

"A powerful spirit our leader summoned from the afterlife. Some of our people found the body of the pig Baka had taken possession of when they went to search for food at the other end of the island. Our leader became enraged when he heard what happened. Baka possesses great magic and his spirit is bonded with Japapa's. They had joined together to drive away the powerful forces attempting to destroy us. Now that Baka's physical presence is no longer with us, there are rumors our leader will be unable to protect us."

"I know you don't trust me. And there is good reason for Japapa to lament Baka's loss. But my father knew a lot about voodoo magic and I might be able to help your leader."

"What can you do?" the guard sneered as Japapa gave out another agonizing scream.

Simone frowned and thoughtfully tapped several fingers against her chin. She had to come up with a plan fast.

"Remember, your leader intends to make me your priestess once we're married. He wouldn't have decided to do that unless he believed I had great powers. My father taught me a lot about voodoo medicine. He was a great priest like Japapa. He even went to Africa to study the roots of our religion. Not only will my powers be useful to Japapa, but I could also be helpful to both of you."

"What kind of help could you offer us?" one of the guards asked suspiciously.

"You never know. My powers could bring you wealth beyond your wildest dreams."

"So, you say. What was your father's name?" one of the guards asked, eyeing Simone with distrust.

"Claude Joseph. He was a professor at the university."

"I've heard of him. He was an enemy of our priest. It was because of him that Japapa was forced to flee Haiti. Why would you want to help?"

"I can see now that my father was wrong about Japapa. When your leader explained to me his plans to help the Haitian people, I realized how much better life would be for all of us. I believe he is a good man. I think maybe I can develop a potion that would drive out the evil spirits that are tormenting him, and it would convince Japapa how willing I am to support his cause. I believe he's under the spell of an evil old woman I met on the boat, and if I don't do something soon to reverse her spell, Japapa might die."

"What old woman are you talking about?"

"A priestess I met on the boat when we were fleeing Haiti. Her name is Mama Atabei. She said horrible things about Japapa and swore to get revenge against him for abandoning her on a deserted island. I stole this from her." Simone held up the plaid flannel sack and removed the amulet inside so the guard could see it. "She told me it had great magical powers and she intended to use it against Japapa. I stole it from her and now that I have it, I can use it to help our leader."

"Let me see that," the guard snarled and wrenched the amulet out of Simone's hand.

"Maybe it would be better if I gave it to Japapa. I'm sure he would know how to use its powers better than you," the guard grunted.

"Maybe. But I'm the only one that can make the potion that will save Japapa, and I'll need the amulet to place a spell over the brew. If I don't do that the potion won't work," Simone explained.

"And just what is this powerful potion made of?" the guard snapped before reluctantly shoving the charm back into Simone's hand.

"Sea urchin eggs and special herbs that grow on the island. They're not very hard to find, and it won't take long to put it together. I spotted several of the plants growing along the trail leading to this hut. It'll take less than an hour to gather up the things I need. Once I've collected them, I'll bring them back to the hut and brew the potion over your fire."

"What do you take us for, a pair of fools?" the guard sneered and gave Simone a suspicious look. "We're not letting you go anywhere. If we agree to let you do this, one of us will gather the things you need and bring them back."

"I'm afraid that won't be possible. Neither one of you know what the plants look like and you might make a mistake and pick one that's poisonous. If this is going to work, I need to be the one doing the collecting."

The stocky guard rubbed the stubble on his chin and frowned. "She might be right," he said to his companion.

"If you won't let me go out alone, you could both tag along while I collect the herbs and urchins."

"I don't trust her," the lanky guard grumbled.

"I don't either, but it can't hurt to let her make the potion."

"I guess. Suppose she concocts a brew that'll kill our leader?"

"We'll make her drink part of it before she gives it to him," the second guard chuckled. "If she doesn't get sick or die, we'll know its safe."

"I'd be happy to do that," Simone agreed. "But we must hurry. If Japapa doesn't get the potion soon, he'll die."

"All right, but you're not getting out of our sight." Grabbing hold of Simone's arm, the burley guard yanked her away from the hut's entrance. "And I'd think twice about pulling any funny stuff."

Staring back into the guard's eyes, Simone realized it was now or never; there wouldn't be any second chance to escape.

CHAPTER

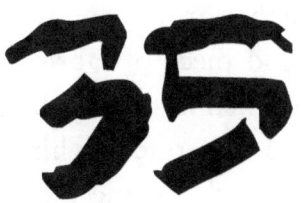

Colonel Hill Police Station, Crooked Island

"De good news is dat de remains of de hand and arm we found attached ta de raft don't belong to your son," the police chief said as Emily and Ben Jenkins let out a sigh of relief. "It belongs to de pilot. I suspected it might be his especially after de fisherman found some of his remains in de shark's stomach."

"Why didn't you let us know your suspicions sooner?" Emily asked.

"I wanted ta wait until it was confirmed by de lab in Nassau. Dey were able ta examine it as soon as it arrived and called me with de results earlier today."

"Does this mean that you think Wendell might still be alive?" Ben asked.

"Yes. After we left Goat Cay, the scientists conducted a more thorough search and found evidence of a campsite. In addition, dey also found dis piece of shirt. Can you tell me if it belongs ta your son?"

Taking hold of the plaid cloth, Emily's hands began to tremble.

"It's his." Ben put his arm around his wife and reached over to take the tattered piece of fabric from her hand. "He was wearing this shirt when he left the house."

"I believe someone has rescued him." The police chief reached over and took back the piece of cloth from Ben and placed it in a clear plastic bag. "It could have been Reggie, de other boy we're looking fer. If dat's de case, der's a chance he'll drop him off on Crooked Island. It's also possible dat one of de fishermen from de Acklins might have found him. I only hope it wasn't one of de Haitians living on de north end of Fortune Island.

"Why's that?" Ben gave the chief an inquiring look.

"Dey are a nasty bunch—nothin' but cutthroats and thieves. Der leader is a self-proclaimed voodoo priest called Japapa. I've been trying to capture him for years, but every time I've planned a raid on one of his camps, he's eluded me. I'm pretty sure he's using drug money ta pay off some of our local officials ta keep him informed about our attempts ta round him and his men up."

"What'll happen to our son if they've captured him?" a despondent Emily asked.

"Dat's hard ta say. Hopefully, nothing serious. Dey often use refugees fer slave labor."

"How soon can you find out if Wendell is with them?" Ben asked.

"Not long. I'm checking with one of my informants later today. I've also ordered a drone from Nassau with a camera ta fly over de camp and see if we can spot him. I know it's hard, but you'll just have ta be patient. In de meantime, let's assume dat he's been rescued by Reggie or somebody else."

"Let's hope," Emily prayed.

"I suggest we make a trip to de south end of Fortune Island. Der's an old hermit who lives der. De locals call him Sharkman. He knows quite a bit about what's going on in dis area. If we're lucky, he might have some information about your son or know someone who does."

"When can we leave?" Emily asked as she tightened her grip on Ben's hand.

"First thing in de morning. Be at de Landrail dock at 7:30. Lewis Garland will also be joining us."

CHAPTER

36

Leaving the South End of Fortune Island

"Where are we going?" Wendell asked as he struggled to keep up with Sharkman and Reggie. His bruised body ached with every step as they raced along the winding trail that led to the other side of Fortune Island.

"To my boat," Sharkman panted. "It's anchored in a protected cove in Danger Bay. We'll use it to get to one of the islands south of here. I set up a camp there years ago. It was our primary base of operation when I hunted sharks."

"How do you know der isn't someone living der?" Reggie asked as he and Sharkman waited for Wendell to catch up.

"I don't. But it's the closest hiding place I can think of, and I don't believe Japapa knows about it." The old man wiped away the sweat on his brow and motioned for Wendell to hurry.

"I knew we should've left that creature alone," Wendell panted and complained after he caught up with Reggie and Sharkman. "Now look at the mess we're in."

"Go ahead, blame me," Reggie pouted.

"That's enough! It isn't going to do us any good for you two to argue amongst yourselves. We need to get to my boat as soon as possible. Look across the water; you can see it at the south end of the bay, anchored near that large cluster of rocks."

Peering across the moonlit bay, Reggie spotted the silhouette of the twenty-foot fishing vessel rocking gently on the incoming swells. "I see her," Reggie acknowledged. "She's bigger dan I expected."

"There were times she didn't seem big enough." Sharkman admitted. "Especially when we hooked large sharks."

"Can we get going?" Wendell asked. "I think we're being followed."

Reggie gave Wendell a quizzical look and shook his head. "What makes you think dat?"

"Because I hear something moving around in those bushes behind us. Whatever it is, it's making a lot of scratching sounds and it seems to be getting closer."

"There's no one following us," Sharkman chuckled. "It's just some land crabs. Go over and check it out."

"A-are you sure?" Wendell stammered.

"Sure, I'm sure. There are thousands of them on this island. They prowl through the underbrush at night searching for food."

"Der's one now," Reggie grinned as a large, gray, spider-like creature moved to within two feet of Wendell and raised it claws. "My dad and I used ta go out at night and catch dem. We'd put dem in a pen, fatten dem up and eat dem fer dinner. Dey are really tasty."

Stepping away from the crab, Wendell stared at the creature and blushed. "I guess I'm feeling a bit edgy after our last encounter with Baka."

"Well, Mon, it's good ta know dat nothing is following us. For a second, you had me thinking it might have been one of Japapa's men."

Further down the trail, the bushes in front of the trio stirred and this time Sharkman motioned the boys to stop. "What is it?" Wendell whispered. "Another crab?"

"It's too big to be a crab." Curious, Sharkman approached the bushes and cautiously looked behind them with his flashlight.

"Do you see anything?" Wendell asked.

Sharkman knelt down, pushed some brush aside, and examined the ground. "Nothing."

"It's probably just a goat," Reggie suggested.

"I don't think so." A puzzled look spread across Sharkman's face. "There are no signs of goat droppings or animal tracks."

"Over there!" Wendell whispered anxiously. "Something just moved out from behind those trees."

"What is it?" Reggie whispered back as he peered into the darkness and tried to make out what Wendell was pointing at.

"I don't know, b-but it's awfully big and it's not human," Wendell stammered.

The grotesque form of an eight-foot-tall monster stepped out on the trail; the lower part of its body had the hooves and legs of a goat while its upper torso was human with horns protruding from its head. Both Reggie and Sharkman stared at the creature in disbelief.

"It's Baka!" Sharkman shouted. "I recognize its demonic form from pictures I've seen in books. Head for the boat!" Sharkman urged as the parrot on his shoulder panicked and took flight.

It didn't take too much convincing to get Wendell moving. Despite his injuries, he fled down the trail in blind panic, tripping over a tree root as he fled.

"Get up!" Reggie yelled. Dragging Wendell out of the brush he'd landed in, the two of them staggered towards the beach as fast as they could.

"We're dead meat," Wendell shouted in terror. Turning his head, he could see the enormous red-eyed form of the demon getting closer.

"Over here," Sharkman yelled, pointing to a narrow passage in the rocks.

"I'll never make it," Wendell gasped.

"We've gotta," Reggie shouted.

Wendell grimaced and nearly fainted as the two of them struggled to reach the water. Behind them, the monster's horrific screams grew closer.

"How far do we have to go?" Wendell groaned.

"Not far," Reggie replied.

Plunging into the ocean, Sharkman and Reggie dragged Wendell away from shore.

"Where's de boat?" Reggie sputtered as he turned around and stared at the ferocious spirit glaring at them from the water's edge.

"Only another couple hundred feet," the old man panted. "But I think we're safe. I don't believe it will follow us out here."

"Well, I'm not taking any chances," Reggie cried. "I'm getting as far away from dat monster as possible."

Gripping Wendell's arm, Reggie frantically began swimming towards the boat. With Wendell in tow, it seemed to take forever to get to the vessel and Reggie began to wonder if he'd ever make it. His arms ached, and when he reached Sharkman's boat, he didn't have the strength to hoist himself on board. Treading water, he anxiously waited for Sharkman to catch up. It seemed it was taking the old man an eternity to reach the vessel, and he didn't know how much longer he and Wendell could stay afloat.

"Hang on!" Sharkman panted when he finally pulled up alongside Reggie. "I know you're struggling to stay afloat, but I need a moment to catch my breath; then I'll hoist myself on board and give both of you a hand. It'll just take me a minute or two."

"I'll try, but I don't know how long we can stay afloat," Reggie sputtered.

"You have to!" Sharkman grunted as he pulled himself into the boat. Once aboard, he leaned over the side, hauled both boys into the boat and collapsed. Too tired to move, the trio stared back at the beach. The creature was pacing back and forth, emitting blood-curdling howls.

"Beware of Baka," the parrot squawked as it landed on Sharkman's shoulder.

It was a warning none of them needed to hear.

CHAPTER

37

Shoreline Near Japapa's Camp

"Over here. Shine your light along the edge of the cliff," Simone urged the guard. "I can see some of the plants I need attached to those rocks about four feet below us. Those and the urchins that live in the tide pools are the last things I need to make the potion."

"Where are they?" the lanky guard asked, kneeling beside Simone.

"Over there," Simone pointed and leaned over the jagged lime rock cliff that ran along the trail.

"I still don't see them." Panning the cliff with a beam of light, the guard tried to locate the plants Simone was pointing to. "Are you sure they're there?"

"I'm certain. You almost had your light on them. Lean over just a little bit further and move your light to the left."

Barely able to keep his balance, the guard extended his body over the edge of the cliff and pointed his light in the direction Simone indicated. "I still can't see them."

"There," Simone shouted. Leaping to her feet she used both hands to shove the guard over the edge. He didn't die quietly. His screams drowned out the roar of the surf as he plummeted towards the beach, his body bouncing off the jagged lime rock protrusions before being swallowed by the ocean.

Fear surged through Simone's body. She was certain the guard's cries had attracted his companion's attention. What would she tell him?

"He slipped," Simone cried hysterically when the second guard arrived. "It was horrible. He lost his balance while we were trying to get some plants."

"Don't give me that," the guard snarled and grabbed Simone's arm. Using his light, he panned the base of the cliff to see if he could locate his companion. "I told you, no tricks!" And he yanked her away from the edge of the precipice.

"I'm not playing any tricks," Simone sobbed. "Let go of me. Please. You're hurting my arm!"

"That's not the only thing that's going to hurt when I get through with you," the guard snarled and pushed her ahead of him down the moonlit trail. "I'm taking you back to camp. I'll have enough to explain when I get back."

"But what about the urchins and remaining plants I still need to collect? If I don't make the potion, Japapa will die. What difference can a few more minutes make? I feel terrible about what happened to your friend, but it would be better for both of us if I can finish what we set out to do. It'll be a lot easier to explain your friend's death, and Japapa will consider it a small price to pay when we save his life."

"Perhaps." The guard glared at Simone suspiciously. "I'll let you get the urchins and the extra plants, but I'm not taking any more chances. While you were gone, I found a place to collect urchins a short distance from here, and I'm sure you can find the rest of the plants you need along the trail without reaching over the edge of the cliff. Come with me. And no more tricks."

Pulling Simone along by the arm, the guard dragged her down the rocky path to a short stretch of beach surrounded by a lime rock outcropping. "Here. You'll find plenty of urchins attached to the rocks near the shoreline," he grouched. "I'll be watching your every step, so get what you need and be quick about it."

"I could use your help." Simone rubbed her aching arm and wiped away a tear.

"I told you before—no more tricks. You can get them yourself."

"All right. But I'll need something to pry them off the rocks."

"Use a sharp rock or a shell. There're plenty of them by the water's edge, and here's a sack to put them in."

Gingerly making her way along the base of the cliff, Simone bent over and picked up one of the rocks.

"Hurry up," the guard grumbled.

"I'm hurrying." Simone stood up and staggered towards the bed of urchins before falling down.

"What's the matter?" the guard growled.

"I twisted my ankle in a hole. It hurts." Reaching down, Simone stopped to rub her leg.

"Get going. I can't believe you're hurt that bad."

"How would you know?" Simone gave the guard a pained look and pretended to wipe some tears away. When she reached the urchin-filled pool, she began prying some from the rocks while the guard paced back and forth.

"Can you help me carry them back?" Simone asked when she finished.

Grumbling, the guard came out to get the sack of urchins and was greeted with a carefully aimed rock that landed squarely against his forehead. Staggering backwards, he fell to his knees. With little time to waste, Simone threw away the sack of urchins and plunged into the ocean.

"You'll regret this," the guard shouted. Lifting himself to his feet, he peered across the moonlit water and tried to determine where she'd gone.

Frantically swimming away from the rugged shoreline, Simone paused for a moment and watched the guard enter the water. He hadn't spotted her yet, but it wouldn't take him long to discover where she had gone. She needed a plan, but her options were limited. The lime rock cliff to her right offered no escape. Its jagged shoreline would cut her to pieces. Her best solution was to surprise him by turning around and heading towards the sandy beach a short distance away. However, it was important that she get there before the guard realized she'd changed direction, and in order to do that, she'd have to swim most of it underwater. Taking several deep breaths, she dove below the surface and headed towards the beach.

Simone's lungs were about to burst when one of the large swells hoisted her to the surface and propelled her towards shore. Tumbling over in the surf, she found herself clawing at the wet sand trying to prevent the receding wave from dragging her back out into the ocean. "I see you," the guard shouted.

Lifting herself up, Simone staggered up the beach looking for someplace to hide.

"This way," the priestess's familiar voice beckoned.

"Where are you?" Simone called out.

"Over here." Stepping out from behind a cluster of dwarf cedar trees, the old woman motioned to Simone. "Follow me. I see you've found a way to escape. This trail will take us to one of Japapa's boats. It's anchored on the other side of the island."

"How did you get out of the cave?" Simone asked before stumbling over a tree root.

"More questions." The old woman sighed. "If I were you, I'd save my breath. Your guard may be stupid, but I don't think he's that stupid. It'll only take him a few minutes to figure out where you're headed. Hopefully, that will give us enough time to get away."

Simone's was nearly exhausted trying to keep up with the surprisingly spry old woman. More than once she tripped and stumbled. Each time the woman would stop and stare impatiently. It seemed like an eternity before they reached the protected cove and stepped out onto the beach where the boat was anchored.

"Can you see the boat?" the old woman asked.

"Yes," Simone panted.

"It has an outboard motor attached to it. Have you ever operated one?"

"Yes, my family had a small boat like it in Haiti. We used it to go fishing."

"Good." The priestess anxiously looked back across the path they had just followed. "The guard will soon be here. You need to swim for the boat."

"What about you?" Simone asked.

"Don't worry about me. I can take care of myself. I've left you a map in the boat's storage box. You can use it to find your way to Crooked Island. You'll find your family there."

Five minutes later, Simone lifted herself on board the boat and quickly located the storage box that contained the map. Inside was a leather pouch with a folded piece of paper, but she would have to wait until daylight before she could read it. Moving to the back of the boat, she hooked up the gas line to the engine, pulled out the choke, pumped on the rubber bulb, and yanked the pull cord. The engine sputtered to life just as a series of terrifying screams arose from the beach. There was no doubt the screams she heard belonged to the guard. A cold chill ran down her spine as she pulled up the boat's anchor. She needed to get away from this place as soon as possible. Hopefully, it wouldn't be long before she was reunited with her family.

CHAPTER

38

Sharkman's Camp, South End of Fortune Island

"He's not here." The police chief stepped outside Sharkman's hut, scratched his head, and walked towards Wendell's parents and Reggie's uncle. "From de looks of things, I'd say he left last night. You can still smell de fish he cooked fer dinner. By de number of dirty plates left on de table it also appears he had company."

"Excuse me," the chief's assistant interrupted. "One of de volunteers just radioed back and said dey found de *Sea Star* hidden in a creek about a half mile from here."

"Did dey find anything else?" Lewis Garland asked.

"Dey located a campsite on de beach a short distance from de boat," the assistant acknowledged. "Dey also found some snorkeling gear."

"Have dem bring de gear here so we can have a look at it," the chief ordered. "Would Reggie have any reason ta come ta dis island?" the chief asked Lewis Garland.

Lewis took a moment to ponder the chief's question and nodded. "His father was going ta buy land out here. In fact, his family was headed ta de bank ta fill out some forms and make a down payment on it when dey were killed in de crash. It's funny I didn't think about dis place sooner. I guess it should have been one of de first places I checked out."

"Here's de gear," one of the chief's heavyset volunteers panted when he reached the dune area where everyone was standing.

"Where exactly did you find it?" the chief asked.

"At de base of a tree about a quarter of a mile from de camp."

"Do you recognize de gear?" the chief asked Lewis.

"Yeah." Lewis shook his head again. "It's Reggie's. His father bought two sets of fins and snorkels a couple of years ago. Dey did a lot of spear fishing together."

Curious about the gear, the Jenkins walked over to have a look. "If Reggie rescued Wendell, why did he bring him here instead of taking him to Crooked Island?" Emily asked.

"I'm afraid I know why," Lewis sighed. "I suspect Reggie didn't want anyone ta find out where he'd run off ta and was afraid Wendell would tell someone if he took him back ta Crooked."

Ben gave the chief a curious look. "So, what about this person they call Sharkman? If Wendell and Reggie met up with him why didn't he bring them back?"

"Good question." The chief scratched his chin thoughtfully. "The fact dat dey appeared ta have left so quickly makes me think dat someone's after dem."

"Who?" Emily asked.

"My guess is dat dey are being chased by Japapa and his men. It's hard ta say why dey are after dem though. Japapa may consider Sharkman a threat ta his operation, although it's hard for me ta think why. As I said before, Japapa and his men are a nasty bunch. If I were Sharkman, I'd head south. Der are lots of small islands in dat direction. Sharkman knows he can't outrun 'em. His boat is way too slow ta do dat. He'll probably head ta one of his fishing camps. Dey could stay der until he figures out what ta do."

"Any idea which camp he might go to?" Ben Jenkins asked.

"Guana Cay is my best guess. It's about five miles south of here."

"The chief suddenly became distracted and began staring out at the ocean. "What are you looking at?" Emily asked.

"Bubbles, Mrs. Jenkins—lots of tiny bubbles. Dey are collecting on de surface about fifty yards out.

Peering into the glare of the early morning sun, Emily had a hard time spotting them. "I'm afraid they're eluding me."

"Look a little more ta de south," the chief suggested.

"I see them now. Are those the bubbles the scientists were talking about?" she asked.

"I believe so." The chief nodded. "Funny—I've lived in des islands fer most of my life and I've never seen so many. I think it's time fer us ta leave and head south and see if we can catch up with Sharkman and de boys. I have an uneasy feeling bad things are going ta happen, and we appear ta be running out of time."

CHAPTER

Cave Near Japapa's Camp, North End of Fortune Island

"You fool!" Japapa shouted at the guard cringing at his feet. "I counted on the two of you to keep an eye on Simone. I can't believe you let her get away."

"I thought we could help you. The girl said that you were being tortured by a voodoo priestess and that she could develop a potion that would save your life."

"Idiot! Only a moron would believe that story. Do I look like I need help?"

"No. But your screams—we all thought . . ."

"Never mind what you thought. Do I look like someone who is about to die?"

"N-no," the guard stammered, "but we were terrified by the thought of what might happen to you when I heard that someone had killed the pig that Baka had possessed. Give me another chance," the guard begged. "I know I can get her back."

"Get her back!" Japapa roared with laughter. Grabbing the man's hair, he yanked the guard's head back, and stared into the man's terrified eyes. "You fool. You don't really expect me to give you another chance? How can I trust anyone who claims he was attacked by a giant snake while chasing a child? Oh, no. I have much better plans for you. Today, you'll see what happens to someone who fails to carry out my orders. Fortunately, your companion is already dead so I won't have to deal with him."

"Please," the guard gasped through parched lips.

"You sniveling cockroach," Japapa hissed as he flung the man down to the cave floor. "Do you know who the *Bizango* are?"

Numb with fear, the guard stared back at Japapa unable to speak. He knew he'd heard of them. Then he remembered. They were the sorcerers of the living dead. What awaited him was grotesque. Struggling to his feet, he staggered towards the cave's entrance in an attempt to escape but was knocked to the ground by the priest's assistant.

"I see you recall them now," Japapa laughed and ordered two of his guards to grab his prisoner. "I've spent years learning their secrets, and now you'll learn how well I've perfected their techniques. Take him outside and give him a shovel," the priest commanded.

Sweat poured from the prisoner's tortured face as he removed the last of the rocks from his shallow grave. Leaning over, Japapa grinned at his captive. "It looks like you need a drink," Japapa chuckled and watched the guard tremble and fall to his knees. "I have just what you need. I brewed it this morning when I decided upon your punishment. It's a tasty brew made from the liver and backbone of the puffer fish."

Seizing the terrified prisoner, the two guards bent the young man's head back and pinched his nose shut. Unable to breathe, the man's mouth opened and the moist concoction slid down his parched throat. Within minutes, the paralysis began to take effect. Soon he couldn't move his arms and legs, but he could see and hear. Bending over and staring into the man's frightened eyes, Japapa grinned and whispered, "I hope you enjoy being buried alive. In a couple of days, you'll be resurrected as a zombie."

CHAPTER

Open Waters in the Acklins Bight Near Guana Cay

"Why did you lie to me?" Sharkman asked.

Folding his arms against his chest, a resentful Reggie stared back at the hermit. He didn't feel he owed the fisherman any explanation.

"You had no right to keep Wendell hostage. What you did created a lot of problems for a lot of people including your uncle and Wendell's family. In addition, there are probably dozens of folks who have spent the past week trying to find both of you. And what about his family? They're probably worried sick. They're thinking he's dead or seriously injured. What an awful ordeal to put them through. And all because you didn't want to move to Nassau to live with your aunt?"

Reggie stared defiantly at the old man, pursed his lips, and shook his head. "I don't care what you or anyone else thinks. It wasn't your family dat was killed. Besides, you're not my father. You have no right ta tell me what ta do."

"You're right. I'm not your father. But I can make sure as heck that Wendell's returned to his parents." Sharkman shook his head and stared at the defiant young man with disgust. "If Japapa's men weren't after us, I would have taken both of you back to Crooked Island today. However, his people would be sure to spot us if we headed north. Worse yet, I hate to think about what will happen to us if Baka hunts us down. He'd probably turn us into something worse than dog meat. Our best hope is to dodge between these islands and hide at my camp on Guana Cay. While I'm there, maybe I can figure out a way to safely turn both of you over to the local police."

After hugging the shorelines of several nearby islands, Sharkman veered his boat southeast over a short stretch of open water. "Land ho," the bobbing parrot squawked. As both boys scanned the horizon, the bird pranced back and forth across the bow of the old man's boat, its green and yellow wings fluttering as if it was about to take off.

"Is that Guana Cay?" Wendell asked when he spied a spot on the horizon.

"Yes, my camp is situated in a cove on the north side. I used to hunt sharks in the surrounding waters. Years ago, they were plentiful throughout the year. In the summer, the females would enter the deep channel at the north end of the island to give birth to their young."

As the boat drew closer, Reggie caught sight of a large shark approaching. Thankful for the distraction, he pointed it out to Wendell as it swam closer.

"It's a female," Sharkman acknowledged before maneuvering the boat closer to the reef. "There are very few males in these waters at this time of year."

"What kind is it?" Wendell asked. Stepping away from the side of the boat, he felt a wave of renewed fear when the creature darted towards them and swam under the boat.

"It's a bull shark. You can tell by their short and broadly rounded snouts. They're abundant in this area. When I first hunted sharks here, I used to use a long line. It was about a mile in length and had hooks attached to it about every ten feet or so. During the dry season we'd catch both the males and females, but in the spring I noticed that I only caught females. We only ever kept the males. I later observed that the females lose their appetites when their young are born. I suppose it's one of the ways nature protects the pups."

"What makes dis place so special dat dey come here ta give birth?" Reggie asked when another curious shark scooted towards them.

"Food, mostly. There's plenty of fish and crabs for the pups to eat inside the lagoon."

After passing through a narrow channel in the reef, their attention was drawn to a flurry of feeding activity taking place near the surface. The black tipped fins of several small sharks sliced through the waters of the grass flats as a silvery school of juvenile bar jacks leapt out of the water. "Dinner is being served," Sharkman said grimly. Stopping the engine, he and the boys watched the frantic life and death struggle draw to its inevitable conclusion as the boat drifted towards the beach.

"It's horrible." Wendell shuddered and tried to blot out the scene taking place in front of him. "People will never be safe as long as animals like this live in the ocean."

"I disagree," Sharkman responded with a shake of his head. "Only a very small percent of people ever get attacked by sharks. These creatures are just doing what they need to do in order to survive. I told you before—you must learn to share this world with other life forms, even ones you don't like."

"So, you say. You didn't see how the sharks ripped apart the pilot."

"No, I didn't. I imagine it was gruesome. However, people like Japapa are even more dangerous than sharks. Unlike sharks, which feed mostly on marine life, people like him kill people just to satisfy their own greed."

"I guess," Wendell grudgingly admitted.

"We're headed to that sand spit," Sharkman said. "If you want to do something constructive, you can anchor the boat and see that it doesn't drift off while Reggie and I check out my campsite."

"All right," Wendell muttered. "How long will that take?"

"Not long. The camp is only about a half mile from here. If everything checks out, we'll be back in less than an hour and make preparations to move in."

After securing the boat, Wendell began slinging shells across the water. "I'll never have any sympathy for those creatures," he mumbled to himself while he watched another school of black tips begin feeding offshore. Hundreds of small, silvery bait fish again flashed through the water attempting to escape their ravenous pursuers. Many did not survive the slashing teeth of their attackers and the shallow flats soon became dotted with small patches of blood. "Killers," was the only word Wendell could use to describe them.

The sun was nearly overhead before the feeding frenzy ended. Surprised by the amount of time that had elapsed, Wendell turned around to see if he could spot Reggie and the old man. They were nowhere in sight. They had been gone longer than Sharkman indicated. Worried that something might have happened, he decided to head inland to find his companions. He didn't have to go far. He was greeted at the crest of the dune by Sharkman's worried face.

"I was beginning to think that something might have happened to you. Is everything all right?"

"I'm afraid not." Sharkman motioned Wendell to head toward the boat. "The gasoline I stored at the camp is gone and the building's been destroyed. It looks like it was torn apart by the last hurricane."

"So, what do we do now?" Wendell asked before turning around and following Sharkman and Reggie back to the boat.

"Head south. I have another campsite on Castle Island," Sharkman said. Pushing his boat away from the shore, he instructed Wendell and Reggie to climb on board. "It's stocked with plenty of fuel and supplies. I'm certain Japapa won't look for us there."

"Why's that?" Wendell gave Sharkman a curious look as he clamored into the vessel.

"Because the local people think the island is haunted."

"That's weird. Did you ever see ghosts when you and your friends camped there?"

"No, but it is a very strange place. As often as I visited the island, I've never seen any lizards or nesting birds."

"What about *Chogers*?" Reggie wanted to know. "Could dey have taken possession of de island? You told us before you were worried about dem showing up on Fortune Island."

"Interesting that you should mention that. Some people think they have, but I've never seen any signs of them. When I think back, one of my friends did say he observed a strange mist rising from the ocean when he was exploring the south end of the island. I didn't think too much about it at the time. I just thought it was fog. When I went back with him to look, it had disappeared."

"What if that camp has been wiped out by a hurricane?" Wendell asked.

"Not likely," the old man responded before turning the key and starting the engine. "The campsite is located in a cave beneath an abandoned lighthouse about a quarter of a mile from the beach. When tropical storms and strong cold fronts passed through the Bahamas and we had nowhere else to go, my crew and I could always count on staying there. It's helped us survive some pretty rough weather."

"How far ta Castle Island?" Reggie inquired. "I don't think I've heard about dis lighthouse before."

"Around fifteen miles, maybe less. I checked the fuel gauge; I'm sure we have enough gas to get there."

"Look out!" Wendell yelled as a large wave almost tossed their boat into the nearby reef.

"No problem," the old man shouted as he maneuvered the vessel away from the cresting waves.

"Mon, did you see dat?!" Reggie pointed to a small boat plummeting into a deep trough.

"See what?" Sharkman asked.

"Der's another boat out der."

"Where? I don't see a thing." The old man shielded his eyes and peered across the turbulent surf in an effort to find it.

"Over der! On de port side," Reggie shouted.

"I see her too," Wendell yelled.

"I've spotted her," Sharkman acknowledged. Turning the bow into the waves, the old man guided it towards the floundering boat. "It looks like a young girl draped over the side. One of you grab hold of the bow line and attach it to the other boat. We need to tie up to the vessel before we get pushed against the reef."

"I've got the line," Wendell yelled.

"Good. Pass it over to Reggie so he can hop on board the boat and tie it up to my vessel. We don't have much maneuvering room and we're getting awfully close to those coral heads."

"I've secured de line," Reggie cried out after jumping into the floundering boat, "but I think it has a hole in de bottom. It's taking on a lot of water."

"Is the person on board ok?" Sharkman asked.

"I don't know," Reggie yelled. "She's not moving. I'm going ta drag her ta de bow and pass her over ta Wendell."

"Careful," Sharkman cried out. "I'm having a hard time keeping us away from the reef."

"I'll be okay," Reggie assured him.

Before Reggie was able to reach the young girl, he was hurled to the deck of the sinking boat. After lifting himself up, he crawled up to the girl and checked to see if she was alive.

"Is she ok?" Wendell shouted.

"She's got a pretty bad gash on her head, but she's still breathing," Reggie yelled. "I'll lift her up and pass her ta you."

"Great," Sharkman cried out as another wave swept them closer to the reef.

While maintaining his balance, Wendell reached over the side of the vessel and tried to take hold of the girl. "Can you keep the boats closer together?" an anxious Wendell asked Sharkman.

"I think so."

As the two boats rubbed alongside one another, Reggie lifted the girl into Wendell's outstretched arms and shouted. "Have you got her?"

"Yes!" Wendell replied as he and the girl were suddenly flung backwards to the deck of Sharkman's boat by another cresting wave.

"Look out!" the old man yelled. "Her boat's about to go under. Cut the bow line, Wendell, otherwise we'll go down with it. Reggie! Get ready to jump!"

As Wendell cut the line, Reggie leapt towards the hermit's vessel just as a large wave pulled the two boats apart. Astonished, Reggie was flung into the water and found himself being swept away.

"Can you see him?" Sharkman cried out to Wendell.

"No."

Anxious moments passed as Sharkman and Wendell peered into the turbulent surf trying to spot Reggie as their boat was carried closer to the reef.

"There—on the other side!" Wendell pointed and shouted.

"I'm okay." Reggie gasped as his head bobbed above the surface. "Someone throw me a line."

"Take hold of this life ring," Sharkman shouted while maneuvering the vessel away from some coral heads. "Wendell can drag you aboard."

After Wendell hoisted Reggie onto the boat, an exhausted Reggie stared at the young girl. "Who do you think she is?" he asked.

"My name is Simone," the girl moaned before rolling her eyes and fainting.

CHAPTER

Acklins Bight, South of French Wells

"Sorry, but I just received orders ta return ta Landrail," the police chief announced as he slowed the engines so the Jenkins and Garland could hear him. "Dat group of Haitian refugees I told you about has been rescued from an island near French Wells. Some of dem are severely injured, and I was asked ta help make arrangements ta transport dem ta a hospital in Nassau."

Trying not to show her disappointment as they broke off the search, Emily asked the chief if he often encountered Haitian refugees.

"Yes, thousands of dem make der way ta de islands each year. Some stay, while others try ta reach de States. Most are trying ta escape from de squalor and wretched living conditions in Haiti. Dis was especially true after de last earthquake. Der were no homes fer dem ta return ta, only crowded camps."

"Dis group evidently had de unfortunate luck of booking passage with a dishonest captain who set dem adrift once dey reached de Bahamas. Most of dem made it ta Cape Flamingo, but den were apparently attacked by Japapa's band of cutthroats who took some of de women back ta de priest's camp. Except for some of de men, de rest were able ta escape. Fortunately, dey were spotted by one of de search planes. Otherwise, we might never have found dem, and many of de older and less fit would have died."

"I'm glad you found them," Emily said. "The sad thing is they won't get a chance to start a new life."

Thinking about his own ancestors and the trials they'd endured to get to the United States, Ben Jenkins asked the chief if there was anything he and his wife could do to help.

"Nothing I can think of. De people in Nassau are working with Bahamas Air ta see if we can get some seats fer de seriously wounded on de next plane leaving Crooked. Some volunteers are trying ta locate nurses ta look after de others. I regret having ta break off de search just when we seemed ta be getting so close. If everything works out, we should be able ta resume tomorrow."

A look of despair spread across Emily's face. "Is there any way we could carry on by ourselves?"

"No, der's no telling what might happen if you ran across Japapa. I know it's hard ta stop looking at dis point, but I think it would be best fer everyone. I believe de boys are in good hands. Sharkman knows des waters better dan anyone. I doubt very much Japapa and his men will catch up with dem.

187

In de meantime, why don't you and your husband try ta get some rest."

Ben frowned and nodded. "I just hope you're right about Sharkman. From your description of Japapa and his band of cutthroats, the boys might be in serious trouble if he captures them. I know you said the priest was not likely to harm Wendell but I'm not so sure that will be the case."

The chief hoped he was right about Sharkman and the boys as well. Staring at the distraught faces of Lewis Garland and the Jenkins, he knew he would never forgive himself if something happened to them.

CHAPTER

42

Sharkman and Teens Arrival at Castle Island, Acklins, Bahamas

"*Qui es-tu?*" Simone groaned and tried to lift herself up.

"What did she say?" Reggie asked.

"She's speaking French. She wants to know who we are," Wendell said. "I learned some French in school. *Parlez-vous* English?" he asked.

"*Oui*—I mean yes," Simone groaned and rubbed her head.

"Good. I'm Wendell. The others are Sharkman and Reggie. Reggie pulled you out of the boat just before it sank. You've been out for a while. You fainted when we dragged you on board."

"How come you speak French?" Reggie asked.

"My father taught me." Simone grabbed the side of the boat and tried to stand up. "Everyone in my family speaks

French, Creole, and English. Most of my people in Haiti speak Creole, but my father said it would be more useful if we spoke all three languages—especially if it ever became necessary for us to escape to another country."

"What are you doing out here all by yourself?" Sharkman asked.

"Trying to escape from an evil voodoo priest named Japapa. You're not part of his gang are you?" Simone asked with a look of apprehension.

"No way," Wendell laughed. "We're trying to get away from him too. Why is he after you?"

"He wants to marry me. His thugs attacked my people and shot my father. I escaped, but one of his henchmen lured me to his camp by telling me my mother and younger brother were with a group he had rescued. He lied and said that the police were responsible for the attack. Like a fool, I believed him. It was only after he took me back to his camp that I learned that Japapa's men were the raiders. Japapa held me captive in a cave and then moved me to the bridal hut in preparation for a wedding ceremony."

"You're fortunate you escaped. How did you accomplish that?" Sharkman asked.

"The guards watching the hut thought Japapa was being tortured by some evil spirit. That evening you could hear the priest's screams throughout the camp. I told the guards I knew a lot about voodoo medicine and that I could concoct a potion that would save his life. They believed me, and when they took me out to collect the plants and urchins I said I needed to make the potion, I escaped. My wedding is supposed to take place later today."

"Pretty clever," Wendell admitted.

"Japapa is ruthless and he won't waste any time trying to get you back," Sharkman said while guiding the boat through a narrow channel in the grass flats. "You'll need to come with us. The only way you'll be safe is with the police."

Simone shook her head and sighed in frustration. "I hope you won't turn me over to them. My parents were hoping to make it to the United States and move in with my uncle. If you take me to the police, I'm sure they'll ship my family and me back to Haiti. If that happens, our lives will be in just as much danger there as they are here. Japapa has great influence in Haiti and I'm sure he'll hunt us down and kill us."

"I'm afraid I don't have any other choice. They're the only ones who might be able to protect you. Besides, they might be able to help your family get asylum in the Bahamas."

"I guess. I only wish that things would have turned out differently. My family spent everything they had to get this far."

"I wouldn't give up hope." Wendell placed a comforting hand on Simone's shoulder and offered her some water. "Things might turn out a lot better than you think."

Simone looked over at Sharkman with tear-filled eyes. "How soon before you take me to the authorities?"

"Not today. We're headed to Castle Island to pick up some gas and supplies. I also need time to figure out a way we can get to Crooked Island without Japapa's men spotting us. If they do, they'll bring us back to their camp and kill us."

In the distance, several jagged bolts of lightning lit up the horizon followed by low rumblings of thunder. "We'd better get going." Without saying anything further, Sharkman increased power to the boat's engine, veered the boat away from some coral outcroppings, and headed south. "The cave where my supplies are located is just below the lighthouse at Castle Island. It's about an hour from here. We need to get there before this squall catches up with us."

Four-foot waves were slapping against the side of the boat when Sharkman and the youngsters reached the island. Stinging sheets of rain pelted their faces, and the salt spray spewed from the wind-generated waves made it almost impossible for them to see. As they got closer to shore, Sharkman shouted at Reggie to throw the anchor over.

"Once Reggie secures the anchor," Sharkman shouted, "I want everyone to hop over the side and wade into the beach."

"I don't know if I can," Simone groaned. "I'm still pretty groggy."

"We'll help you," Reggie urged after the anchor grabbed hold of the bottom. "Once you're in de water, Wendell and I will guide you ta shore. Take my hand and we'll jump in together."

Simone hesitatingly grabbed hold of Reggie's hand and grimaced as they leaped over the side.

"Where's Wendell?" Simone sputtered when her head bobbed above the surface.

"Right next to you," Wendell yelled. "Grab my hand and we'll wade ashore together."

Once he saw the youngsters make it to the beach, Sharkman turned off the boat's engine and joined them. "Take that path through the rocks," he shouted.

The blinding rain made the narrow, winding trail difficult to follow and the slippery rocks on its surface made for treacherous footing. Simone and Wendell lost their purchase several times and slipped backwards before righting themselves.

"I can see de lighthouse just ahead," Reggie yelled excitedly as he pulled himself over a rocky ledge and staggered towards it.

"Good, look for the cave entrance beneath it," Sharkman panted. "Once we're inside, I'll start a fire to dry our clothes."

Stumbling into the cave, Reggie collapsed onto the ground with Wendell and Simone close behind.

"Did you see him?" Wendell gasped.

"See who?" Reggie asked.

"Baka. I'm certain I saw him staring at as us from behind those rocks when we entered the cave."

"I sensed something too," Simone added.

"I didn't see a thing," Reggie sighed. "If we're lucky, we'll never see him again."

"What's the matter?" Sharkman asked the boys as he entered the cave.

"Wendell thinks he spotted Baka's spirit beside some rocks near de entrance."

"I know I did," Wendell retorted.

"Well, I doubt he's followed us here." Sharkman took a minute to think about it then stepped outside to make sure. "The rain is making it pretty hard to see, but I'm certain he's not out there."

Wendell wasn't sure at all, however. During the last burst of lightening, he was absolutely positive he saw Baka's demonic presence move behind some trees and heard the creature laughing at them.

CHAPTER

Colonel Hill

"Has anyone found my daughter?" Claude Joseph asked from his police stretcher. Hovering next to him, his worried wife and son looked on with concern. "We got separated during the attack," he gasped. "Her name is Simone—Simone Joseph."

"We haven't found her yet, but we're doing everything we can ta locate her," the police chief promised. "Your wife can give us a description and tell us where she might be hiding. Right now, you need ta get some rest. We're sending you ta a hospital in Nassau where dey can treat your wounds."

"You mustn't take too long," Claude said frantically as he tried to lift himself up. "She may have been captured with some of the other girls by the band of thugs that raided our camp," he groaned as tears ran down his face. "If they have, there's no telling what they'll do to my daughter"

"Please, Mr. Joseph, you need ta remain still. You've lost a lot of blood." A nurse stepped in front of the police chief and gently pushed Joseph back against the stretcher. With a nod of her head, she signaled two Nassau policemen standing close by to lift him up and carry him to the plane.

"I'll have my assistant and a group of volunteers look fer her and de rest of de girls dis afternoon," the chief promised as Claude was loaded onto the plane. "If dey can't find dem on Lucian Cay, we'll check out de smuggler's camp tomorrow morning."

Marie Joseph and her son watched in despair as the plane revved its engines and taxied down the runway for takeoff. The fear of never seeing her husband and daughter again was foremost in her mind when the chief motioned for them to follow him.

"He'll be all right," the chief promised as the plane took off and he led her away from the runway. "We have excellent teams of doctors in Nassau. I'm sure he'll be up and around in no time."

"I hope you're right," Marie said. Wiping the tears away from her cheeks, she watched the plane disappear into the clouds. "I guess you would like a description of my daughter."

"Yes."

"I had a number of photographs taken of us before we left Haiti." Reaching inside her pocket Marie pulled out several crumpled pictures and handed them to the chief. "This is a close-up of my family. That's Simone with her arms around our family dog. If for some reason one of us didn't make it,

I wanted the rest of us to have some way to remember each other."

The police chief smiled and looked at the photograph. "Your daughter is a beautiful young girl."

"I'm glad you think so. Is there any hope of finding her?"

"I'm sure der is. Why don't you come with me ta Landrail. You and your son can get somethin' ta eat at Mrs. Gibson's. She operates the best restaurant on de island."

"Thanks." Marie smiled and opened the back door to the chief's jeep so her son could climb in. "I'm not really hungry, but I'm sure Michael is famished."

"You can't neglect yourself," the chief said. A look of concern spread across his face. "It's important dat you regain your strength. Your husband and children will need you."

"I guess, but everything seems so hopeless." Marie sighed and stared out the jeep window as they left the airport parking lot. "Even if our family gets together again, your government will send us back to Haiti. There's nothing there for us anymore. My husband is a marked man. His enemies assassinated one of his friends before we left and they threatened to kill him. That's why we took off for the States. If we go back, I doubt he'll survive more than a week, and God only knows what will happen to the rest of us."

"I understand." The chief nodded and gave Marie a sympathetic look. "Perhaps I can work something out so you and your family won't have ta go back. What did your husband do in Haiti?"

"He was a history professor at the university in Port-au-Prince. He was well-respected and admired by his students."

"I have some friends in de government. It just might be possible dat I could find him a job in de Bahamas. Our country could use an educated man like Mr. Joseph."

Marie didn't respond to the chief's suggestion. There were too many other things to think about, and the likelihood of anything good happening didn't seem promising.

That night, after dinner at Mrs. Gibson's, the chief updated Reggie's uncle and Wendell's parents about the searches. "While I was dealing with de Haitian refugees, some fishermen were still looking fer Sharkman and de boys at his fishing camp on Guana Cay, but der was no one der. Seems dat de camp was severely damaged by a hurricane. I also sent some people ta look fer some of de Haitian girls on Lucian Cay. Dey made a thorough check of de island and found nothing. De more I think about it de more likely it is dat Sharkman, de Haitian girl, and de boys have been taken ta Japapa's camp. I intend ta raid de camp tomorrow morning. Some of de Nassau police will be helping, and I feel certain we'll rescue de rest of de refugees and have your children back in your hands shortly."

After listening to the details of the chief's plan, Wendell's parents and Reggie's uncle asked if they could join the raiding party.

"I can't allow dat," the chief said. Looking over at their anxious faces he knew he would want to do the same if he were in their shoes. "Der might be shooting and you could be seriously injured."

"I know," Lewis Garland said, "but I thought we should at least make de offer."

"I recognize dat," the chief responded. "However, I'd like you ta remain here at de station during de raid. I'll keep you informed about what's happening through de police radio."

Disappointed, the group nodded in agreement and left the office. The best thing they could do now was pray the chief would successfully rescue everyone.

CHAPTER

Japapa's Hut, North End of Fortune Island

"Who's there?" Japapa bolted upright in his cot and looked around.

"Don't you recognize me?"

The priest squinted at the shadowy figure in the corner of his hut. Glaring back at him was Baka's demonic form.

Rubbing his eyes so he could see more clearly, a trembling Japapa staggered to his feet and confronted Baka's demonic presence. "You must forgive me; the hut is dark and I did not recognize you right away. I wasn't expecting to see you so soon. It appears your efforts to eliminate the two boys were not successful."

"You're correct. I was about to kill both of them when the old hermit interfered."

"I know. My men informed me it was the shark fisherman that killed the wild boar you took possession of."

"The three of them were more resourceful than I anticipated. I pursued the trio to Sharkman's boat but they escaped and headed south. When I tried to get a good handle on where they were headed, the priestess clouded my vision making it temporarily impossible to locate them. It's also come to my attention that you are looking for the young Haitian girl, Simone. I thought you captured her and were making wedding arrangements."

"Yes, but she escaped. I'm certain that the priestess helped her get away."

"Do you know where she is?" Baka asked.

"No, I planned to resume looking for her in the morning. Now that I know the boys and Sharkman escaped your clutches, my men and I will look for them as well. Do you have any idea where the girl might be?"

"As a matter of fact, I do. A fisherman was more than eager to tell me after I applied a little demonic persuasion. He spotted Sharkman and the boys rescuing Simone and heading south to Castle Island. I've since located them in a cave on the island and have been keeping watch over them."

"A clever place for them to hide," the priest noted. "With all the superstition surrounding that place, I would never have looked for them there. Now that I know where they are, my men and I will get together and immediately head out after them."

"That would be wise," Baka smiled. "The fisherman also informed me that there is going to be a raid on your camp."

"Did he say when?"

"No. But I wouldn't take all of your men with you. Leave some to take the Haitian women you captured and set up camp on another island. Once you have Simone back and have taken care of Sharkman and the boys, you could rejoin them. I suggest moving your operation to Inagua. It's further south and there are fewer police there to interfere with your smuggling business."

"Sounds like a good plan. I can promise you, Sharkman and the youngsters will be in our hands by the end of the day, and I'll make certain they pay for what they did." Shouting for his assistant Peter, Japapa began making plans to capture and kill Sharkman and the boys and make preparations for his wedding.

"I can see that you're anxious to get started so I'll leave you to your preparations. But remember our agreement; I intend to hold you to your promise," Baka hissed. "Failure is not an option. If you don't live up to your end of our bargain, I'll see that you pay a terrible price."

The threatening tone in Baka's voice made Japapa tremble. It was a bargain with the devil and he would be roasting in hell if he failed. Wiping sweat from his brow, the priest felt a wave of fear run down his spine as he watched Baka's satanic form fade into the darkness.

CHAPTER

Coastal Waters Near Japapa's Camp

A new day was about to begin. The sun had lifted its head above the horizon and the humid morning air was saturated with the sweet smell of night-blooming jasmine.

"Should we begin de operation?" the chief's assistant asked.

"Not yet. I'm not comfortable with what I see."

"What do you mean?"

Scanning the camp with his binoculars for the second time, the chief pursed his lips and shook his head. "Der's been no activity around de camp since we arrived. Dey may be waiting ta ambush us."

"Do you think someone told dem we were coming?"

"It's possible. Japapa has a lot of informants in de islands. De priest pays dem a lot of money fer information. Signal de

Nassau reconnaissance teams ta move ashore and scout things out and let me know what dey find."

More than an hour passed without any word. Pacing back and forth across the deck of his small boat, the chief asked his assistant to contact the away team. "What's taking dem so long?" he grumbled.

Before the assistant could pick up the transmitter, a voice came over the radio. "No sign of Japapa and his men, Chief. De only ones here are an old woman and some of de kidnapped Haitian women. De old woman said de guards intended ta take de rest of de women ta another island but dey took off when der lookout spotted our boats approaching."

"Is Simone with dem?" the chief asked.

"No."

"Is der any sign of Sharkman and de boys?"

"Not so far."

"Damn," the chief mumbled to himself. "Okay, I'm headed ashore. Do de women have any idea where Japapa and his men have gone?"

"No, dey don't seem ta know very much. Dey heard Japapa tell his men ta set up a camp on Inagua and have one of der group meet up with him and tell him where de new camp is located. My people are questioning de old woman now. Hopefully, she'll be able ta give us more information by de time you get here."

"Let's hope so." Turning off his radio, the chief instructed his assistant to head toward shore.

There was no wind, and a mid-morning layer of heat blanketed the camp by the time the chief stepped ashore. Wiping the sweat from his face as he approached the young man in charge of the away team, he asked, "Has de old woman given you any more information about where Japapa's headed?"

"Yes, sir. Castle Island."

"Do you know why dey chose dat island?"

"She probably does, but she specifically said she would only talk ta you, dat you were de only person she trusted."

"Where is she?"

"In the cave at de top of de hill. I'll take you."

"Lead de way. We're running out of time. If Japapa captures Simone and de others, der's no telling what he'll do with dem."

When they reached the cave entrance, the reconnaissance team leader motioned the chief to stop. "It's pretty rank in der, sir. If I were you, I'd cover my nose before you step inside."

As the chief entered the cave, he pulled out his handkerchief and placed it over his mouth and nose. Gingerly moving forward, he felt his breakfast about to reappear when the smell of rotting flesh overwhelmed him. But it was the cockroaches that bothered him the most. They were scurrying everywhere. He could hear the hissing sounds produced by their legs as they ran across the floor and began running up his pants legs and crawling across his chest. Brushing them off his arms and face, the chief called out, "Is anybody here?"

"It's taken you long enough," the old woman chastised.

"I came as soon as I heard you wanted ta speak ta me." The chief stared into the dark recesses of the cave trying to locate the woman. "One of de reconnaissance team members from Nassau said dat Japapa and his men have gone ta Castle Island. Do you know why?"

"To find the people responsible for killing the life form Baka took possession of and fleeing with Japapa's future bride."

"Who's Baka and who's dis person Japapa intends ta marry?"

"Baka is a demon the priest summoned from the afterlife. Sharkman and the two young boys killed the boar Baka took possession of. Now, Baka wants Japapa to seek revenge for what they did."

"And de girl? Who is she?"

"A young Haitian, Claude Joseph's daughter. She was on the ship with the other refugees. You must hurry or you will be too late to stop the wedding ceremony and save Sharkman and the boys."

Stepping near the cave's front entrance, the old woman shook her head and glared at the police chief. Although her body was withered and bent, her green eyes radiated a fiery passion that retained the policeman's attention.

"I'd like ta know more about dis wedding and de sacrifice dat's about ta take place," the chief said. Handing her a crumbled photograph from his pocket and pointing to a young girl, he asked, "Is dis de girl Japapa intends ta marry?"

The old woman held the photograph close to her face, ran a gnarled finger across the girl's image, and gave an affirmative nod. "She'll make a lovely bride, don't you think?"

"M-my God!" the chief stammered. "Dis girl's only a child."

"I agree. But there are girls younger than her who have been enslaved by men like Japapa. This evening, just after the sun sets, her wedding ceremony will begin with the sacrifice of the boy. Afterwards Japapa and his followers will toast the new bride by drinking the young man's blood."

"And de boy—who is dis boy?"

"The one who nearly died in the plane crash, of course."

"You mean Wendell Jenkins?!"

"There is no time for more questions," the old woman sighed. "Japapa and his men are approaching Castle Island as we speak. You must hurry if you expect to reach Sharkman and the children in time."

Shocked by the woman's revelations, the police chief dashed outside the cave and raced down the hill to the beach. Out of breath as he reached the shore, he instructed two of his men to take the Haitian women back to Crooked Island and the rest to follow him to Castle Island. The island was a good distance from the camp, and he knew it would take them a good part of a day to get there. If what the old woman said was true, there wasn't much time left to save Simone, Sharkman, and the boys.

CHAPTER

Open Waters Near Castle Island

"What's happening?" Japapa's Haitian boat captain asked as their fleet of boats passed through a sea of bubbles.

"It's nothing," Japapa responded. Some Bahamians believe that when the sea is covered with bubbles like this it's a sign that the *Chogers* are about to appear."

"What are *Chogers*?"

"Ghosts. Supposedly, they rise out of the mist created by the bubbles and choke people to death. I can assure you it's all a lot of nonsense, a gory tale local parents use to frighten their children when they want them to behave."

"How can you be so sure there isn't some truth to it?" The captain crossed himself and stared apprehensively at the surrounding waters.

"I didn't realize you were religious," Japapa chuckled.

"I'm not, but it's better to be safe than sorry."

"I see. Well, in all the years I've been in the Bahamas, I've never seen any ghosts rise out of the mist and kill anyone. Take my word for it. I'm familiar with the spirit world. The sea fog is our friend. I've used it many times to escape from patrol boats."

"I'm glad to hear that," the captain said as he looked around and took stock of the group of boats following them.

"Have you ever been to Castle Island?" Japapa asked.

"Once, a very long time ago. The place gave me the creeps. When I went there, there were no signs of life and the people that lived at the north end had abandoned the place. There was also something else about the place that made me feel uncomfortable, but I can't remember what it was. I know some of the Bahamians say the island is cursed."

A glimmer of recognition spread across Japapa's face. "Does the island have a lighthouse on a steep hill and a series of protected coves on the opposite side near the south end?"

"Yes, have you been there?" the captain asked.

"I believe so, many years ago. I was looking for a place to set up my drug-smuggling operation. It appears to be the same place my assistant Peter and my crew checked out. Peter knew about the abandoned houses and the lighthouse. When we went ashore, we discovered the body of an old fisherman. He appeared to have choked to death. The really strange thing was his body hadn't decayed and the shock and fear of what had killed him was etched across his face. When we left, I vowed I'd never return."

The captain glanced over at Japapa with a look of concern. "Do you think it could have been the *Chogers* that killed him?"

"No," Japapa laughed. "Besides, I have no intention of turning back now because of some silly superstition. I promised Baka I'd capture Sharkman and the boys and make them pay for what they did. It was clever of the old man to seek refuge on Castle Island. With all the weird things happening on the island and the superstitions surrounding the place, he probably thought we'd never look for him there. If you were him where do you think he'd hide?"

"I'd hide out in the cave at the south end. It's high up on the cliffs and it's a good lookout location. You can see boats approaching through the east channel for miles."

"Is there a way to get there without being seen?"

"There's a hidden cove on the opposite side of the island. The locals on Crooked have told me about it. We can anchor the boats there and hike across to the lighthouse. I understand the underbrush is pretty thick, but I think we can make our way through it without too much trouble."

"Good. Radio Peter, my assistant, and the other boats and tell them our plan. And this time, inform everyone I expect no slip-ups," Japapa snapped. "If any of the children or Sharkman get away, I'll hold them all personally responsible."

The grim look of determination on Japapa's face left little doubt in the captain's mind that the priest meant what he said. His boss never made idle threats, and this was one time he and the others would make sure they lived up to his expectations.

CHAPTER

The Cave on Castle Island

"Wake up," Wendell shouted. "It's time to get going."

"What's de big hurry?" Reggie grumbled as he wiped the crusty sleepers from the corners of his eyes. "Maybe you'll be glad to get back ta Crooked Island, but I'm not. Being sent ta Nassau to live with my aunt and uncle is not my idea of a thrilling experience."

"It might not be as bad as you think." Sharkman yawned and lifted himself up. "It'll be a lot better than sleeping on the rocky floor of this cave and being chased by Japapa and his band."

"Yeah, and the further away I get from Baka the better," Wendell added.

"I know about Baka," Simone said. "He's a powerful spirit Japapa summoned from the afterlife. One of his guards told me someone killed the animal he'd taken possession of."

"That was Sharkman," Wendell responded. "He speared the pig as it was about to kill me. Unfortunately, we haven't seen the last of him. Baka's demonic form nearly killed all of us when we tried to escape from Fortune Island last night. I've never seen such a grotesque creature in my life. It's half-human and half-goat with enormous horns protruding from its head. I'm convinced that his spirit followed us here."

"Der's no way dat happened, Mon," Reggie groaned and lifted himself up. "I never saw his ugly face when I entered de cave and neither did Sharkman."

"I don't care what the two of you think!" Wendell snapped. "I still think he's watching us. I know what I saw."

"Enough!" Sharkman groaned and stretched out his arms. "We don't have time to argue over whether Baka's here or not. We need to get going. I suspect it won't take Japapa and his men very long to figure out where we are. Before I went to sleep last night, I figured out a way to get to Crooked Island without being spotted."

"Swell," Reggie grumbled. "Can we eat first?"

"Later. We can have breakfast on the way," Sharkman said as he reached over and began picking up some of his gear.

"I'm not so sure I like heading back there either," Simone sighed. "The thought of being sent back to Haiti by the police terrifies me."

"I know, but the police are the only ones who can help you find your family," Sharkman said. Handing Reggie the boat keys, he asked him to bring the boat ashore so they could load the extra gas for the trip. "We'll drain some fuel from the storage tanks and join you in a few minutes," Sharkman yelled to Reggie who raced out of the cave with a smile on his face.

After Wendell finished helping Sharkman fill up the gas cans, he carried a couple to the front of the cave. A refreshing easterly breeze greeted him as he made his way down to the boat. There wasn't a cloud in the sky, and Sharkman's promise to get him to Crooked had revitalized his spirits. Soon he would be back home with his family. It wasn't until he reached the beach that his outlook changed. Both Reggie and the boat were gone. "Now what's he done?" Wendell groaned.

"Looking for someone?" Japapa chuckled as he stepped out from behind one of the bushes and grabbed Wendell's arm.

CHAPTER

48

Castle Island

There was a big grin on Reggie's face as he headed north with Sharkman's boat. There was no way he was going to let that old fisherman bring him back to his uncle so he could spend the rest of his life in Nassau. He had gassed up the boat just after everyone had gone to sleep and had intended to sneak off before daybreak. Oversleeping almost foiled his plan. He couldn't believe his luck when Sharkman gave him the keys and sent him to bring the boat ashore. Now, he was free. It wasn't until he rounded the point of Castle Island that he spotted a fleet of small vessels anchored in a cove on the other side.

There was no doubt that the boats belonged to Japapa and his men. Looking around, he spied a small creek. Maneuvering Sharkman's vessel between two rocks, he tied the anchor line around one of the mangrove trees and pondered his options.

Ever since he'd made plans to move to Fortune Island and fulfill his father's dream, nothing had gone right. First, there was his untimely discovery of Wendell and what to do with him. Then Baka and Sharkman complicated things, and they had to leave Fortune Island only to encounter Simone. Now his plan to strand Sharkman and the others here on Castle Island and retrieve his own boat didn't look like it was going to work. Initially, it was his intention to sail to Crooked Island and leave a note for the police telling them where Sharkman, Wendell and Simone were. But it was obvious that would be a problem. Japapa and his men were already on Castle Island, By the time the police got here, Japapa would have killed Sharkman and Wendell and forced Simone to become his wife. His only choice was to find a way to save them. But how? He had no weapons. Whatever he decided to do, it had to be done fast; otherwise, his companions were toast.

CHAPTER

The Cave on Castle Island

"No one escapes from me," Japapa growled at his captives. "First, I want to know which one of you delivered the fatal blow to Baka. My men told me it was you, old man. And did this sniveling boy help you?"

When no one responded, Japapa stepped closer to the trio and snarled, "Perhaps you didn't hear me?" Grabbing Wendell's face, he glared into his eyes. "I might even take pity on you and let you have a painless death if you tell me the truth, or was it the boy who escaped with your boat, Old Man? Oh yeah, it was silly to trust him. My men are out looking for him now. I can assure you he won't get very far."

There was more silence as Wendell stared back through tear-filled eyes.

"What a pity you'll have to die so young," the priest laughed as he pushed Wendell to the cave floor. "And what about you, my beauty?" Japapa whispered into Simone's ear. "Can you tell me which one of them did it?"

Shaking her head, Simone trembled as the priest placed his burly hand against her cheek.

"There's no reason to be afraid," Japapa assured her. "In a few hours, our wedding ceremony will begin and you and I will be joined together as husband and wife."

"I don't want to marry you!" Simone sobbed and pulled away from the priest. "You're nothing but a disgusting animal."

"What a pity you feel that way. After a while, I'm sure you'll change your mind. Just look at the beautiful gown my men plundered from one of the many refugee ships that passed through these waters. I brought it with me just for the occasion. It's made of pure silk. I assure you the young woman they took it from will no longer have any use for it."

"You're disgusting," Simone yelled and kicked dirt on the dress. "I have no intention of wearing that. It makes me want to puke when I think about what your crew probably did to that poor young woman."

An annoyed look spread across the priest's face as he motioned to one of his guards to take Simone away. "See that she's dressed in that gown for the ceremony," he growled. Turning towards Sharkman, the priest laughed, "And what should I do with you, Old Man?"

Glaring at the priest, Sharkman spat in his face. "Yes, I killed the pig that Baka took possession of. So why don't you let the boy live?"

"Your concern touches me," Japapa sneered. "But I can't disappoint my followers. The wedding ceremony demands a sacrifice. We'll drink your young friend's blood. I can't think of a better tribute to our gods. It's a shame you won't be there to enjoy it."

In horrified disbelief, Wendell staggered to his feet when he heard Japapa's plans. His eyes darted towards the cave's entrance hoping to find a way to escape, but two of the priest's guards stood in the opening. Realizing it was hopeless, he fell to the cave floor and began to sob. A wicked roll of laughter echoed off the cave walls as Japapa looked over at him. "Don't worry, my little sniveler. I've decided to make death quick," the priest snarled and motioned to his men to take Wendell away. "On the other hand, I've prepared a special treat for you, Old Man, one that will be certain to please Baka."

CHAPTER 50

Waters South of Fortune Island

"How much longer before you reach Castle Island?" Ben Jenkins asked the police chief over the radio. He'd just listened to the chief retell the old woman's story and now was more anxious than ever about the safety of his son.

"About three hours. I was hoping we'd get der sooner, but it took longer dan I expected ta get our boats refueled at Landrail. Japapa and his men have at least a half day's head start."

"That means you won't get to the island until late afternoon," Ben observed after a brief pause.

"I'm afraid so. Don't lose hope. Now dat I know exactly where dey are, I'm sure we'll be able ta rescue dem."

"And what if you don't?" Emily asked.

"Dat won't happen. I promise you we'll get everyone back unharmed."

"Let's hope so," Ben conceded. "Please continue to keep us informed."

"I'll try, but we're going ta maintain radio silence from now on. We don't want any of Japapa's men listening ta our communications. I'll notify you as soon as de rescue has been completed."

It's going to be difficult to carry out the operation during daylight, the chief thought as he terminated radio communications with the families. The chief knew Japapa's lookouts would be posted by the time he and his team arrived. His best hope was to approach the island through the mangrove swamps at the north end. The terrain in that area was rugged, but it was less likely that the priest would expect an attack from that direction. Timing would be everything. Anxious to get to the island, he turned to his boat operator, "Can you go any faster?" From the look he received, he knew the answer was no.

CHAPTER

Castle Island

As he hid behind some rocks, Reggie observed two men guarding the cave's entrance. There was no doubt they were Japapa's thugs. Slipping closer so he could get a better look, he waited to see what would happen. It didn't take long. There was muffled laughter inside the cave as the priest stepped outside and instructed two of his guards to take Wendell and Sharkman away. Shoving them along the rocky trail that led to the far side of the island, one of the men kicked the old man in the rear and urged him to hurry up. "Some of Japapa's men are waiting for you," he snarled as the other laughed.

"Where does Japapa want us to take the boy?" the guard asked.

"To the altar," his companion chuckled. "Japapa will deal with him later."

Grabbing Wendell's arm, one of the guards pulled him towards a large clearing where the wedding festivities were being set up. "I'm sure you're anxious for the ceremony to begin," he laughed as he tied the boy to a tree.

The other guard scowled at Sharkman. "Too bad you'll miss the event. Our leader has more interesting plans for you. Arrangements are being made aboard his boat as we speak."

Reggie had seen Japapa's fleet of boats anchored in the lagoon when he made his way across the island. He suspected he knew exactly where they were taking the old man, and from what he had observed in the lagoon, the torture they intended to inflict on him was gruesome. Finding a shortcut through the underbrush, he raced ahead of the guards and made his way back to where the fleet was moored.

Loud laughter greeted him when he arrived at the site. Peering through the bushes, he saw the priest's vessel tied up to an old wooden dock with several crewmen throwing chunks of bloody fish over the side. "Give them more," one of them shouted.

"Man, they sure are hungry." The crewman grinned before tossing another chunk of meat into the water. The entire crew seemed mesmerized by the lather of pink foam that spread across the lagoon. There were sharks everywhere. Stirred to a feeding frenzy, the surrounding waters had become a boiling cauldron of death.

The vision of Sharkman being eaten by these ravenous creatures turned Reggie's stomach. Looking around, he spotted a large wooden boat pole near some trees. That might be just what he needed. Sneaking closer, he grabbed the sturdy pole and waited behind some bushes for the guard and the old man to show up.

Anxious moments passed. Then one of the crewmen spotted Sharkman being pushed down the dock. "Just in time," he laughed. "We've almost run out of food for our friends."

The guards grinned. "Well, we've brought them a special treat. Do you think they're ready for this tough old morsel?"

"I doubt it. He's not as tender or as tasty as the fish we've been feeding them," one of the men chuckled.

"That's too bad. But I don't think they'll notice the difference. Tie him to the end of the boat's boom and we'll lower him slowly into the water."

"Wouldn't it be easier if we just tossed him over the side?" one of the men asked.

"I'm sure it would be, but those weren't my orders. Our leader wants him to suffer for what he's done."

Nodding, one of the crewmen stepped forward and dragged the old man onto the boat. "Tie him to a rope and swing him over the side," the guard commanded.

Hanging upside down over the water, the old man stared into the boiling cauldron of sharks and waited for his life to end.

CHAPTER

Goat Cay

Geologist Jan Larsen had a worried look on her face. After reviewing her findings with fellow scientists, she shook her head in disbelief. She never thought something like this could happen. Like her colleagues, she felt that the release of high amounts of methane gas in the Bahamas was just another fanciful explanation for the disappearances that were supposed to have taken place in the Bermuda Triangle.

Now she knew differently. The bubbles that local residents reported rising to the surface were coming from huge deposits of gas trapped beneath the bottom sediments. They were much larger than the smaller pockets they expected to find. And when she put together a map of where the bubbles were surfacing, they formed a straight line from French Wells to Inagua, and it appeared that Castle Island was at the epicenter of the release. In addition, the seismographic readings she'd recorded over the last twenty-four hours showed that there was going to be a huge underwater landslide near Castle Island in the imminent future. This would be catastrophic to any shipping in the area.

"How soon do you expect it to happen?" the head scientist, Jack Nance, asked after reviewing her findings.

"Within the next couple of hours. It's hard to say. One thing is certain. We need to warn everyone to steer clear of the waters around Castle Island."

"Agreed," Nance acknowledged. "I'll contact the authorities and ask them to alert local residents living near the landslide about the danger and put a call over the radio for anyone who might be fishing in the region. In the meantime, get our cameras ready. After I make the calls, I'll get 'hold of the airport and have them send a company chopper to get us. It should only take them an hour to get it here. When the underwater slide happens, I want to make sure we record the event."

CHAPTER

Castle Island

"Look out!" the guard yelled as Reggie scrambled aboard the boat and lunged towards them with the wooden boat pole hoisted above his head. Turning around just in time to see the crazed expression on their attacker's face, both men were caught unprepared and hurled into the water.

Reggie never heard their screams because a guard grabbed him by the arm and yanked him backwards. "You'll pay for that!" he growled as Reggie tried to free himself. Lifting Reggie off his feet he glared into his face and laughed. "Those sharks won't mind having a little something extra to eat," he snarled.

That moment of hesitation was all that Reggie needed. Lunging forward, he clamped down on the man's nose with his teeth and held on for dear life. It worked. The guard staggered backwards and threw Reggie to the deck. Knocked dizzy when his head slammed against the gunnel; Reggie found himself still clenching a piece of the man's nose firmly between his teeth as he slowly recovered his senses.

"You're finished," the enraged guard screamed as he reached for his knife.

Spitting out the guard's nose, Reggie rolled over, barely eluding the razor-sharp blade that whisked past his throat. A second swipe of the knife nicked his ear and Reggie suddenly found himself back up against the boat's gunnel.

"There's no place for you to go now." The bloodied guard grinned before stepping forward to make a final thrust with his knife.

Reggie cringed and closed his eyes. Lunging forward, the guard catapulted past him into the frothy cauldron of hungry sharks as terrified screams followed.

Amazed that he was still alive, Reggie opened his eyes and stared at the blood and squashed nose lying on the deck. Fortunately for him, the man had slipped on it and was flung overboard when he made his final lunge. Still trembling, but thankful he wasn't dead, Reggie staggered to his feet and turned towards Sharkman.

"Get me down!" the old man yelled.

"Hang on!" Reggie shouted. Stumbling towards the winch, he grabbed its handle and pushed with all his might. It wouldn't budge.

"Try harder," Sharkman pleaded.

Once again, Reggie tried to get the winch to move. To his relief its rusty gears started to turn.

"Forget the winch!" a panicked Sharkman yelled. "The line I'm tied to is about to break. Swing me over the deck."

Looking up with horror, Reggie realized he had only a few seconds to save the old man. The rope had nearly unraveled. Mustering all his strength, he swung the boom over the stern just before the rope snapped. His mouth agape, Reggie watched Sharkman plummet to the deck and grimaced as he landed with a large thump.

"Are you all right?" Reggie yelled.

"I think so." Sharkman moaned. "Fetch a knife and cut my hands loose!"

Grabbing one of the fisherman's knives, Reggie bent down and sliced through the remaining piece of rope.

Rubbing his sore wrists, Sharkman slowly stood up and winced. "We've got to rescue Wendell. They're going to offer him up as a human sacrifice as part of Japapa's wedding ceremony. Let's go! From the sounds of those drums, we don't have much time."

Sharkman and Reggie were nearly out of breath when they planted themselves behind a rocky outcropping near where the wedding ceremony and sacrifice were about to take place. Gyrating dancers chanted praises to a demon whose image hovered above the altar. Every few minutes the drumbeats grew louder and soon the flailing arms and legs of Japapa's followers merged into a single satanic mass.

"What are dey doing?" Reggie stammered.

"I really don't know," an equally astonished Sharkman replied. "I've never seen anything like it. It appears to be their way of honoring Baka."

"It looks pretty sick if you ask me." Reggie shuddered as Japapa stepped out onto the lime rock ledge above his followers.

Waving his arms, the priest shouted to his gyrating admirers for silence. "Today," he began, "with your help, the gods have brought me a bride. Have you ever seen anyone so beautiful?" Japapa motioned to one of his guards who dragged Simone, dressed in a flowing, white silk gown, from behind the ledge and made her stand beside the evil priest. "After we are married, I'll train her in the secrets of our religion and she will become your priestess."

Shouts of joy rose from the group and several of the men began chanting their praises to Japapa.

"Silence!" the priest commanded. "Before the wedding can take place a human sacrifice must be made to strengthen the bonds of this union. In honor of the occasion, I've chosen one of the people responsible for killing the boar that Baka's spirit once possessed. To show respect for Baka, we will drink his blood and pay lasting tribute to the spirit world that protects us."

"Bring him to us!" some of the priest's followers shouted.

Wendell was led to the altar kicking and screaming and forced to stare into Japapa's vengeful eyes.

"What do you want most of all?" the priest asked Wendell.

"To live," he sobbed.

"Then your wish shall be granted," Japapa shouted. "You shall live in the bodies of each person who drinks your blood."

Motioning his followers to come closer, the priest lifted his knife and swept its glistening blade toward Wendell's throat as he lay stretched across the altar.

CHAPTER

A Clearing on Castle Island

"What about de radio message?" the police chief's assistant asked. "The geologists said der could be an underwater landslide near Castle Island within de next couple of hours and our lives could be in danger."

"We'll just have ta take de chance dey are wrong," the chief said. Everyone was out of breath when they entered the clearing on the island. "I promised de relatives I'd bring der children back, and I don't intend ta fail dem. Let's head ta de place de old woman told us about and be quick about it."

Racing to the place where they heard the chants of Japapa's men, the chief and his crew arrived just as the priest was about to slit Wendell's throat. Shouts of surprise broke out from Japapa's followers and an expression of disbelief spread across Japapa's face when several Nassau policemen raced towards him.

"We got ta do something," Reggie yelled above the anguished shouts of Japapa's followers. "De police will never be able ta reach Wendell in time."

Before Sharkman could grab him, Reggie raced towards Japapa, jumped onto the lime rock ledge, and yanked Wendell away just before the priest's knife swooped down to cut Wendell's throat.

"Look out!" Simone shouted.

Once again Japapa's knife flashed through the air and this time penetrated deep into Reggie's shoulder. Stunned by the force of the blow, Reggie fell backwards and lost consciousness.

Frozen with fear, Wendell hugged the ground as Japapa pulled the blade from Reggie's shoulder and lunged towards Wendell's neck.

"No!" Simone screamed and hurled herself at the priest's legs, knocking him off balance. Cries of frustration followed as Japapa's knife struck the ground inches from Wendell's body. "Follow me!" she shouted and grabbed Wendell. Barely avoiding the priest's outstretched hand, Wendell stumbled to his feet and staggered into the underbrush with Simone.

"You won't escape," Japapa snarled. "I'll find you wherever you go."

"Look out!" one of the priest's followers yelled. From the corner of his eye, Japapa spotted one of the police chief's men about to grab him.

"Head for the boats," Japapa shouted while knocking the policeman to the ground. Lumbering through the bushes with his bodyguards beside him, the priest was gasping for air by the time he reached the water's edge. There was no time to waste. The police were closing in. Struggling into the nearest boat, Japapa ordered his boat captain to start the engine and head out to sea.

"Don't let dem get away!" the chief shouted as his officers raced after the fleeing smugglers.

Bullets whizzed past Japapa as the rest of his followers clamored into their vessels and took off.

"It's no use!" a frustrated Nassau policeman cried out as he watched Japapa's boats head south. "Our vessels are on de other side of de island. We'll never catch up with dem."

"Radio our people anyway. We might get lucky," the chief shouted.

"I doubt it," his radioman replied, "but I'll radio dem."

"Damn," the chief grumbled in disgust. "Has anyone seen de children?"

"Over here!" Wendell and Simone shouted.

"Thank God. Where's Reggie?"

"Back in the clearing. He's hurt bad," Simone said. "He needs a doctor."

"I'll have de medic get him."

"No need for that. I've got him," Sharkman panted as he staggered onto the beach with Reggie. "I've put a tourniquet on his arm. He's lost a lot of blood."

"I'll take care of him," the medic said reaching for his medical kit.

"Wow! What's that?" Wendell shouted as he turned and pointed.

Looking across the water, everyone stared in disbelief as a strange fog bank swept towards them.

"It's the *Chogers*!" Sharkman gasped and turned pale. "We've got to get out of here. Whatever's in that fog will kill us."

CHAPTER

The Sky above Castle Island

Chief scientist Jack Nance shouted and motioned to the helicopter pilot, "Head towards that fog bank, but don't get too close."

"What is that stuff?" the pilot asked as he turned the chopper in the direction Jack was pointing.

"Methane gas mixed with particles of water vapor. The gas was released from the ocean bottom. If we enter that cloud we'll suffocate. In addition, any sparks from this chopper might set off an explosion. If that happens they won't find enough of us to bury."

"Some people think clouds like this might be responsible for the disappearances that take place in the Bermuda Triangle," Jan Larsen added. "Before it gets too dark we'd like to record this event with our cameras. I wish we had a drone with a camera, but we couldn't get one from Nassau in time. It may be the first time anyone's seen something like this and lived to tell about it."

"Well, I hope we don't become one of its victims," the pilot said as he maneuvered the chopper as close as he could for the scientists to get their movies.

"What's that?" Jan asked, pointing toward a small group of objects moving away from Castle Island.

"A flotilla of boats headed straight into the cloud. I don't believe it!" Jack yelled as he peered through his binoculars.

"Can we warn them?" Jan asked.

"Too late for that." Jack sighed as he watched the boats disappear into the mist. "I thought I warned all the boats in this area about the underwater slide about to take place and what would happen to them if they remained here."

CHAPTER

56

Japapa's Flight from Castle Island

"W-what is that coming toward us?" the boat captain stammered.

"A fog bank." The priest's outlook brightened when he realized he could use the mist to slip away from the police. Laughing with glee, he slapped the captain's back. "The gods are with us. We can use it to hide from the police boats. Head straight for it."

Two hundred feet from the wall of mist they could hear the hissing sound of bubbles breaking on the surface. "It doesn't look like any fog bank I've ever seen," the captain said and nervously looked over his shoulder to see if the other boats were following.

"Me either," another man riding in Japapa's boat gasped.

"I think we should turn back," the captain suggested as he opened his mouth trying to breathe.

Realizing his mistake, Japapa turned towards the captain and motioned him to steer away from the approaching cloud, but it was too late. Wide-eyed and choking, the priest and his followers plummeted towards the ocean floor in a mist-filled envelope of lethal gas.

"I warned you not to fail me," were the last words Japapa heard as Baka's satanic form glared back at him from the foggy bottom. Descending into the darkness, the priest could also hear the old woman's laughter as the light faded from his eyes.

"I've won," the old woman whispered in his ear. "Too bad. Your evil plot has failed. Enjoy your life in Hell."

CHAPTER

Escape to Lighthouse on Castle Island

"Let's go to the lighthouse just above the cave we were hiding in," Wendell shouted in desperation.

"If we can get to the top," Sharkman agreed, "there's several rooms where we can seal ourselves off from this toxic cloud. I'd also tell your men to stop chasing Japapa and head north away from the fog bank."

"I'll have my radioman contact our boats on de other side of de island immediately."

"Follow Wendell and Simone to the lighthouse," Sharkman shouted to the rest of the officers. "The medic and I will carry Reggie."

As the toxic cloud drifted closer, it got more difficult for everyone to breathe. Wendell and Simone were the first to reach the lighthouse followed by the chief and the rest of his men. Looking back, Simone and Wendell could see that Sharkman and the medic weren't going to make it to the lighthouse with Reggie.

"We need to help them, Simone," Wendell urged. "You assist the old man. I'll get the medic and Reggie."

"Okay," Simone agreed.

After reaching Sharkman, they clamored up the rocky slope. Simone and the old man barely escaped the advancing wave of toxic gas.

The medic and Reggie were less fortunate. A few hundred feet from the lighthouse entrance, Wendell and the medic, with Reggie in tow, were desperately gasping for air. Collapsing to the ground, all three passed out.

"Get up." Wendell felt someone grab his arm and urge him to stand.

"Who are you?" he gasped in astonishment as he looked up and spotted an old woman glaring at him.

"A friend," the woman assured him. "I'll get you to the lighthouse."

"All three of us?"

"Yes, I'll instill all of you with the strength you'll need to make it."

"I don't think that's possible," Wendell gasped.

"You'd be amazed at the powers I possess," the woman assured him.

Feeling their strength return and their ability to breathe renewed, Wendell and the medic stared at one another in disbelief. With renewed vigor, they hauled Reggie to the lighthouse and safety.

"We've got you," the chief shouted as two of his assistants dragged Reggie, Wendell and the medic through the lighthouse entrance. "Help dem up de steps ta de top of de lighthouse," the chief ordered. "We'll be safer der."

"Der's not time; we need ta give dis boy CPR right now!" the medic insisted.

"All right," the chief agreed. "De rest of you head ta de top of de lighthouse and seal yourselves off from de toxic cloud. I'll seal de lighthouse door and den help de medic with Reggie."

Reggie's heart stopped twice before the medic and chief got it to start beating again.

"I don't think we can get him upstairs in time," the chief said.

"We've got ta try," the medic gasped. "Let's go!"

Meanwhile, Wendell reached the top of the lighthouse where Sharkman and the others were gathered behind a sealed door. Frantically banging on the metal door, Wendell prayed that Sharkman and the rest would hear him. To his relief, the old man unlatched the entrance and pulled him inside. "Are you all right?" a concerned Simone bent over and asked Wendell as he collapsed onto the floor

"I guess." Wendell groaned and began coughing.

Minutes later, the medic and Reggie made it to the compartment and were quickly dragged inside by Sharkman and the others. Reggie was still in bad shape when he entered the room and everyone was worried that he wouldn't live. "Look! I just found some diving equipment and an oxygen tank that must have belonged to the old lighthouse keeper. Maybe oxygen will help Reggie," Simone offered.

"Great," the medic replied. "What just happened out there?" he asked Wendell as he continued to administer to Reggie. "I felt certain we wouldn't make it."

"Me too," Wendell said. "And we wouldn't have made it back without that old woman's help."

"What woman?" the chief asked. "Der was no old woman outside when we rescued you."

"I saw her. She spoke to me," Wendell insisted. "She gave us the strength to reach the lighthouse."

"I have ta admit I was amazed we regained our strength, but I didn't hear anything," the medic offered. "It was probably just a hallucination. Near death experiences can do dat ta you."

Simone, of course, knew differently.

CHAPTER

58

Nassau, Bahamas

JANUARY 2020

"Where am I?" Reggie groaned.

"A hospital in Nassau." Wendell got up from his chair and moved to Reggie's bedside. "We thought you were a goner. You've been unconscious for nearly three days."

"I feel awful," Reggie sighed.

"I'm not surprised. You lost a lot of blood."

"Are Simone and Sharkman okay?"

"Simone's here. She stopped by a little while ago to see how you were doing. Her father is in a room a few doors down the hall. Sharkman stayed on Crooked Island. He's helping the scientists find more places where poisonous gas is rising to the water's surface."

"Poisonous gas?"

"Yeah. It seems those ghosts he called *Chogers* were really pockets of poisonous gas escaping from the ocean floor."

"And Japapa?"

"He's dead. His boat sank when he tried to get away. All of his men died except for the ones that fled to Inagua. Those that died either choked to death in the cloud of poisonous gas or their boats sank to the bottom of the ocean."

"Dat's good. I'm glad I won't have ta see der ugly faces anymore. Are your folks here?"

"Yes, I asked them to let me stay until you woke up. I wanted to thank you personally for saving my life."

"It was de least I could do," Reggie said. "Besides, I wouldn't be here if it wasn't fer you." Reggie looked out the window. "You know I was going ta leave you on dat island."

"I know. But in the end you didn't. You did the right thing."

"I guess. But Sharkman was right. I was being selfish when I decided ta run away. I owe a lot of people an apology."

"Your apology is accepted," Reggie's uncle said as he and Simone entered the room. "I'm glad ta see you're awake."

Slowly turning his head, Reggie greeted his uncle with tear-filled eyes. "I'm sorry," he said again and sobbed.

"I know." His uncle reached out and squeezed Reggie's hand. "I'm sorry, too. Your aunt and I thought we were doing what was best for you when we decided ta send you off ta live in Nassau."

"I realize dat now," Reggie said. "When I get out of here, I promise I'll move in with my relatives der."

"That won't be necessary," Simone said excitedly. "My dad is alive and he said he wants you to live with us on Crooked

Island. After I told him how you saved my life, he said he wouldn't have it any other way."

"Gee, dat's great, but how can he manage dat? I thought dey were going ta send you and your family back ta Haiti."

"I thought so, too, but the police chief talked to some of his friends in Nassau and got my father a work permit. He's going to be the principal at the new school they're building on Crooked. The chief said everyone on the island was excited about getting an educated man like my father to take over the school."

"If my aunt and uncle don't mind, I'd love ta stay with your family."

"No, we don't mind," Uncle Lewis said with a smile. "And you'll be happy ta know dat de police found de *Sea Star* and brought her back to Crooked. She's tied up ta de town dock in Landrail waiting fer you."

"I can't believe everything turned out so well," Reggie said with a sigh of relief.

"Everything except for the fate of most of our countrymen," Simone added as a look of sadness spread across her face. "Most of them are being sent back to Haiti. I only wish they could stay here with us."

"What will happen to them?" Wendell asked.

"That's hard to say. There's still a lot of unrest in my country. That's why we were leaving. If Japapa had come back to Haiti, it would have just made it worse. Plus, some of Japapa's followers are still there. My guess is that most of the people that are being sent back will try to leave again. I would if I were them. Their lives will be at risk every day they're there."

"Beware of the *Chogers*," the parrot squawked and pranced back and forth on Simone's shoulder.

"Oh, I almost forgot," Simone smiled. "Sharkman asked me to give him to you as a Christmas present. We all thought he was dead, but he flew into the bushes when Japapa's men captured us. Later, a fisherman found him on one of the other islands and brought him to Sharkman. They wouldn't let him stay here with you, so I've been sneaking him in, hoping I'd be able to show him to you when you woke up."

"Hero," the bird squawked before taking flight and landing on the railing of Reggie's bed.

"We agree," Wendell's parents said as they entered the room. "We can't thank you enough for saving our son."

"And my daughter," Simone's mother added.

"Enough is enough." A broad-chinned nurse with narrowly set eyes strode into the room with a scowl on her face. "Someone should have notified me immediately when dis young man woke up. He's been through a terrible ordeal and needs his rest. I insist dat all of you leave right now. You can come back tomorrow during visiting hours, and don't bring dat nasty creature back with you."

Promising to return, everyone reluctantly waved goodbye to Reggie and headed down the hallway towards the stairwell.

"What are you going to do now?" Simone asked Wendell as they exited the building.

"We're going back to New York City the day after tomorrow."

"Do you ever plan to come back?"

"Sure. I've already asked if I could spend next summer with Grandpa. At first, my parents didn't like the idea, especially after what's happened, but I think Grandpa and I convinced them to let me do it."

Simone smiled, "I'll be looking forward to your visit."

"Yeah, me too. Maybe we can do some fishing and snorkeling together."

"That would be fun, but what about your fear of sharks? Your parents told me you had quite a bad experience with them after the plane crashed."

"I did. I watched them attack the pilot and then attempt to toss me overboard. I still have nightmares, but in time, I think I can learn to live with them. Besides there are worse things than sharks to worry about."

"You mean people like Japapa?"

"Yeah. Did you hear what the Nassau police found out?" Wendell said.

"That Japapa may have been responsible for the death of Reggie's parents?" Simone nodded. "Do you think Reggie knows what happened?"

"Not yet. I overheard Reggie's uncle and my parents talking about it in the hallway. His uncle said he wanted to get more details from the Nassau police about what happened before he says anything to Reggie."

"It's going to come as quite a shock," Simone said. "I'm not sure how I'd react to something like that."

Wendell sighed. "Maybe staying on Crooked and living with your folks will help him through the rough spots."

Simone paused and gave a thoughtful nod. "I hope."

"Besides sharks, I'm also having nightmares about Baka," Wendell admitted. "An old woman keeps showing up in my dreams too, and she's constantly warning me about him. I'm certain she's the one who helped the medic and me get Reggie back to the lighthouse."

"I know about the old woman," Simone acknowledged. After passing through the hospital door, Wendell and Simone paused for a moment under the streetlight. "Besides my parents, you're the only other person I've told this to. She helped me escape from Japapa too."

"Do you know who she is?"

"She told me she's a voodoo priestess named Mama Atabei. My father said he never met her, but her followers helped him overthrow the ruler of Haiti that Japapa worked for many years ago. I never believed in voodoo, but after meeting her I'm not so sure. There are too many things about her I can't explain. If I were you, I'd take her warning seriously. When I was on the boat coming from Haiti, she gave me this plaid sack with an amulet in it for saving her life. She said it would protect me from evil spirits, and I've worn it around my neck ever since. It appears that you may need it more than I do."

Lifting the sack from around her neck, Simone placed it in Wendell's hand and smiled.

From across the street, Baka's fierce red eyes glowed in the dark as he watched Simone and Wendell turn the corner and follow their parents to their hotel. *Next summer*, he thought, *will be soon enough to get my revenge.*

www.ingramcontent.com/pod-product-compliance
Lightning Source LLC
Chambersburg PA
CBHW051146030726
47504CB00004B/1071